Patrick Hamilton was one of the most gifted and admired writers of his generation. Born in Hassocks, Sussex, in 1904, he and his parents moved a short while later to Hove, where he spent his early years. He published his first novel, *Craven House*, in 1926 and within a few years had established a wide readership for himself. Despite personal setbacks and an increasing problem with drink, he was able to write some of his best work. His plays include the thrillers *Rope* (1929), on which Alfred Hitchcock's film of the same name was based, and *Gaslight* (1939), also successfully adapted for the screen (1939), and a historical drama, *The Duke in Darkness* (1943). Among his novels are *The Midnight Bell* (1929); *The Siege of Pleasure* (1932); *The Plains of Cement* (1934); a trilogy entitled *Twenty Thousand Streets Under the Sky* (1935); *Hangover Square* (1941) and *The Slaves of Solitude* (1947). The Gorse Trilogy is made up of *The West Pier* (1951), *Mr Stimpson and Mr Gorse* (1953) and *Unknown Assailant* (1955).

BY PATRICK HAMILTON

Fiction

Monday Morning
Craven House
Twopence Coloured
Twenty Thousand Streets Under the Sky
Impromptu in Moribundia
Hangover Square
The Slaves of Solitude
The West Pier
Mr Simpson and Mr Gorse
Unknown Assailant

Plays

Rope
John Brown's Body
Gaslight
Money with Menaces
To the Public Danger
The Duke in Darkness
The Man Upstairs

PATRICK HAMILTON

MONDAY MORNING

ABACUS

First published in Great Britain in 1925 by Constable
This paperback edition published in 2018 by Abacus

3 5 7 9 10 8 6 4

A CIP catalogue record for this book
is available from the British Library.

ISBN 978-0-349-14164-0

Typeset in Sabon by M Rules
Printed and bound in Great Britain by
Clays Ltd, Elcograf S.p.A.

Papers used by Abacus are from well-managed forests
and other responsible sources.

MIX
Paper from
responsible sources
FSC® C104740

Abacus
An imprint of
Little, Brown Book Group
Carmelite House
50 Victoria Embankment
London EC4Y 0DZ

An Hachette UK Company
www.hachette.co.uk

www.littlebrown.co.uk

Introduction

It is a mystery that for many years the work of one of the century's most darkly hilarious and penetrating artists fell into near obscurity. Doris Lessing declared: 'I am continually amazed that there is a kind of roll call of OK names from the 1930s ... Auden, Isherwood, etc. But Hamilton is never on them and he is a much better writer than any of them'.

Recently, however, Hamilton's novel *The Slaves of Solitude* was adapted for the stage, and the films of his taut thrillers, *Gaslight* and Alfred Hitchcock's adaptation of *Rope*, are now considered classics. He is regularly championed by contemporary writers such as Sarah Waters, Dan Rhodes and Will Self.

Patrick Hamilton was one of the most gifted and

admired writers of his generation. With a father who made an excellent prototype for the bombastic bullies of his later novels and a snobbish mother who alternately neglected and smothered him, Hamilton was born into Edwardian gentility in Hassocks, Sussex, in 1904. He and his parents moved a short while later to Hove, where he spent his early years. He became a keen observer of the English boarding house, the twilit world of pubs and London backstreets and of the quiet desperation of everyday life. But after gaining acclaim and prosperity through his early work, Hamilton's morale was shattered when a road accident left him disfigured and an already sensitive nature turned towards morbidity.

Hamilton's personality was plagued by contradictions. He played the West End clubman and the low-life bohemian. He sought, with sometimes menacing zeal, his 'ideal woman' and then would indulge with equal intensity his sadomasochistic obsessions among prostitutes. He was an ideological Marxist who in later years reverted to blimpish Toryism. Two successive wives, who catered to contradictory demands, shuttled him back and forth. Through his work run the themes of revenge and punishment, torturer and victim; yet there is also a compassion and humanity which frequently produces high comedy.

In 1924 Hamilton gave up his job as a shorthand typist, working for a sugar producer in the City of London, and began work on the novel that would become his first work of published fiction, *Monday Morning*. The book went through a number of working titles, including 'Immaturity', 'Adolescence' and 'Ferment'. By the end of the year it was finished.

An introduction via his sister, Lalla, led to the book being taken on by the distinguished literary agents A. M. Heath. After rejections from Jonathan Cape and Heinemann, the rights were bought by the respected Michael Sadleir at Constable, and a very happy personal and professional relationship began. Hamilton received a £50 advance against future royalty earnings. Within a year *Monday Morning* was published to good reviews and in an American edition from Houghton Mifflin. Hamilton's career had begun.

After the success of his second novel, *Craven House*, came *Twopence Coloured*, his witty satire on the theatrical profession, published in 1928.

In the 1930s and 40s, despite personal setbacks and an increasing problem with drink, he was able to write some of his best work. His novels include the masterpiece *Hangover Square*, *The Midnight Bell*, *The Plains of Cement*, *The Siege of Pleasure*, a trilogy entitled *Twenty Thousand Streets Under the Sky* and The Gorse Trilogy, made up of *The West Pier*, *Mr Stimpson and Mr Gorse* and *Unknown Assailant*.

J. B. Priestley described Hamilton as 'uniquely individual ... he is the novelist of innocence, appallingly vulnerable, and of malevolence, coming out of some mysterious darkness of evil.' Patrick Hamilton died in 1962.

"'TIS AN ERROR, SURELY, TO TALK
OF THE SIMPLICITY OF YOUTH.
I THINK NO PERSONS ARE MORE
HYPOCRITICAL, AND HAVE A MORE
AFFECTED BEHAVIOUR TO ONE
ANOTHER, THAN THE YOUNG. THEY
DECEIVE THEMSELVES AND EACH
OTHER WITH ARTIFICES THAT DO NOT
IMPOSE UPON MEN OF THE WORLD'

Esmond.

To Bruce Hamilton

Contents

Chapter One

MONDAY

I

The door was shut fast upon an empty and forgotten room.

It was high up in a high hotel, and its window overlooked a rough sea and a grey sky, and the wind-driven, deserted King's Gardens of Hove.

Many noises came to the room. There was the noise of the sea, pounding measuredly in the lulls of the wind. And the wind moved the window pane to little thuds and rattles. Far below, an errand boy on a bicycle could be heard whistling 'In a Monastery Garden' as loud as he could, louder than he could.

His whistling faded in the wind. Outside the door could be heard a maid at a cupboard. A man dimly hummed and bumped about in an adjoining room.

All the things in the room lay, with a certain silly acqui-escence, exactly as they had been put; save for one of the two Japanese fans in the fireplace, which gave a startling little fall in its newspaper bed, as though it had been listen-ing to all this strange silence for a long time, and had had quite enough of it.

There was a small, white-quilted bed, on which lay folded pyjamas of plain pattern. Over the bed-rail was a highly coloured school tie.

There was a dressing-table, and on this one hair-brush with a handle to it, and a bottle of brilliantine.

There was a washing-stand with ordinary washing things, and a small leather box containing a safety razor and blades – a very new box.

In one corner of the room was a cricket bat, shiny from recent oiling, upside down – a 'Force' bat, with 'J. B. Hobbs' heavily engraved across the splice. The oil was on the mantelpiece with some crested hotel ornaments and a pipe, which had been smoked perhaps three times. Beside this lay two packets of wire pipe-cleaners. One pipe-cleaner had been taken out and used, but was not at all dirty.

And by the bed was a small wicker table. On this a chess-board, a box of chessmen, Staunton's Chess Handbook, Wisden's Cricket Almanack, and 'The Cloister and the Hearth'.

The front cover of the last was open, and there was an inscription on the fly-leaf. This was not an ordinary inscription. It would be gathered from some quaint turns in the phrasing, and the spelling, and numerous elaborate curls and flourishes in the lettering, that the writer was giving his impression of what he thought, perhaps, a very old-fashioned inscription might have been like. It was certainly no success as this.

First, the writer's great, unbridled delight had been to alter each available 's' into 'f,' which peculiarity, to begin with, an old-fashioned inscription never had. And then, having tasted a substitution or two, and found them good, the writer had lost his head quite, and turned even each sibilant 'c' into 'f.'

'Thif book,' it went, 'if the fole property of one Mafter Anthony Charterif Forfter, and waf purchafed by him in the yeare of Grafe One Thoufand, Nine Hundredf and Twenty One, fhortly after leaving Weftminfter Fchool, where he refeived an college education af befitf a young gentleman.

'A moft model young perfon, loved by all hif friendf, refpected by all hif acquaintenfef, and gone in fear of by hif enemief.

'May hif life prove an highly merrie one, and pleafaunt, and fucfefful.'

'Fucfefful' was surely a triumph. The author might have done well to finish on 'Fucfefful.' But he could not forbear one final poke, in the tombstone manner—

'Not gone before but loft.'

Save the pictures, nearly all the things in this room have been mentioned, for it was a bare room.

3

The pictures had been chosen by Anthony Charteris Forster. Along the wall by the bed were five postcard pictures of Kirchner girls, who had tender, slim limbs, and creamy, pampered skins; and they were very dreamy and soft. On the wall above the bed was a large portrait of Mary Pickford. It was a present from the *Picture-goer*. Mary Pickford was seen in a fresh, brown mist, and she looked, with a facetious and provoking indifference, across the room at another picture called 'Off Valparaiso'. This was a fine, deep-blue affair, with a great wind and a stout old ship.

These pictures had plainly been up some time, and the drawing pins which held them to the wall were becoming a trifle rusty. But over the mantelpiece were three very new pictures, and the drawing pins were a bright gold colour. Three pictures – of Shelley, of Byron, and of Keats.

In all the grave patience and stillness of the empty and forgotten room, Shelley and Keats, very properly, were at their Writing. They were not writing just at the moment, but had pens in their hands and gazed out at the wall opposite, in a meditative hunt for the next phrase.

Byron was not at his Writing. He was looking very sternly at Mary Pickford. That gave meaning to all her provoking indifference. Also Byron did not want anybody to miss the fine points of his profile.

4

II

A boy, about eighteen years old, was standing on the steps of a small hotel in Earl's Court.

It was dusk in January, and the subdued Square attended gravely to the noise of some children playing with a great dog in the Square garden. The boy was nervous and depressed. He touched a white button which said 'Press', but heard no answer in the house. He put down his heavy bag and waited. Soon there were clicking noises behind the door, and the door was opened by an untidy man in a shiny blue suit and a begrimed shirt.

'Oh. Gould I see Mrs Egerton, please? She's expecting me, I think.'

'Yessir. Not quite sure she's in, sir. What *would* the name be?'

'Er – Forster,' said Anthony.

Mrs Egerton, the hotel proprietress, and in appearance a hotel proprietress, came and brightly welcomed Anthony. She took him to his room. She showed him the billiard-room, the ball-room, and the dining-room. She told him the time of the meals, and she said 'Nowadays they don't dress for dinner unless they want to.' Then, after laughing instructions for finding his room again, she left him.

He sat on his bed, looking at the twilit window and thinking that Mrs Egerton was a very nice woman. He hoped that he would see her again soon, and she would perhaps introduce him to some people in the hotel; but he had a notion that Mrs Egerton was the sort of person who was wonderful when you first arrived, but afterwards only the person to whom you gave your bill at the end of the week, and with whom you just passed the time of day, if you met her in a passage.

Rising, he switched on the electric light. The bulb was old and dirty and gave out a reddish tinge. He started to unpack his bag, which his aunt had packed for him yesterday. In all places she had screwed, or wrapped, or lain newspaper. Anthony put all this out on to the floor, diving straight for his chessmen and Wisden's Cricket Almanack, which were at the bottom. These he put on his dressing-table. Then he made well-compressed balls of all the bits of newspaper and put them in a drawer, and kicked his bag under the bed. He put his hands in his pockets and looked at the impression of himself in the glass. This was of a person with dependent eyes, a fairly good nose, a very good mouth, and a nice figure. The reddish light was a kind light. Anthony did not like his face. Nor did he feel able to judge his face. It was not a clearly-defined thing, like other people's faces.

He stood for some time looking at the floor with wide, unseeing eyes. Then he ran downstairs to what Mrs Egerton had trained her guests to call the Lounge. This was a sort of hall, and entrance, and centre of the Fauconberg Hotel. It was a fair-sized room, deadened by thick carpets. There was a large fireplace with a black and grey fire, dull red, leather armchairs and sofas, and some small tables. In the centre a palm, and in one corner a woman having tea.

Anthony pretended he was cold, and rubbed his hands in front of the fire. Then he sat down in one of the armchairs and lit a cigarette.

Leisurely, high exploration of absent eyes towards the woman. Sidelong attainment. Sudden sharp meeting of eyes and lightning withdrawal.

Soon the woman gathered her bag and some parcels and left the room. Anthony heard her meet another woman outside, and talk to her. 'Would you really be so kind?' he heard, and 'I really feel quite ashamed for troubling you about it.' Confiding words, laughter, and silence.

Overwhelmingly quiet down here.

'I think I'll go out and get a nice light novel,' thought Anthony. So he ran upstairs for his hat and coat, and came down into the cold night air.

He went to Smith's, bought 'The Lady from Long Acre', by Victor Bridges, and wandered about Earl's Court for awhile. He thought of his aunt, and the things she would be doing at this hour, down at Hove. He saw her sitting alone at their table, choosing her dinner with the agreeable Swiss waiter ...

When he returned to the Fauconberg Hotel bright lights were up in the lounge, and quite a few people were about the fire, which was becoming red. Not wanting to face them, he ran up to his room, paced, decided to face them, came down and sat on a red sofa by himself.

The door of the lounge creaked often now; many people were coming in. They set up a confused, loud mumble, broken by louder laughs. They all looked very brushed and washed, and most of them wore evening dress.

The women were mostly in black lace dresses. A youngish woman stood in front of the fire, with her thin, over-cherished hands bent back in front of the blaze. She asked all as they entered if they would make a fourth at Bridge. Her husband stood by her, a man lavishly reminiscent of Lord Carson. He had just given up his armchair to an old lady who knitted and talked to him, looking, with a contortion, over her spectacles. There was a pretty girl of about twelve, double in an armchair, with a big book, scowling at it. Everybody made bluff remarks to her; she looked up to smile for a polite length, but was soon scowling again. There was a girl of about twenty-three, nearly pretty from a special and rather infrequent angle. There was a moustached, vigorous young man in good tweeds, who looked like a man in an advertisement for an expensive pipe tobacco.

All about were conversational centres for Bridge, Dancing, 'The Beggar's Opera', Setting up as a Dressmaker, The celibate disposition of the Prince of Wales, The Differentiation between Einstein and Epstein, The Adventure of Mrs Jackson with a Rude 'Bus Conductor. The wife of the Lord Carson man told a young man that she would tell his mother about him. One of the knitting old ladies said that she thought his mother knew.

And frequently there would be the clicking noise of a key at the front door, and young men with double-breasted blue overcoats would come in; they were tired, untidy, office-dirty, and they went upstairs.

People were very near Anthony now, crowding him out, talking across him. So he lit another cigarette. Then he had to bring an old letter from his pocket and read it carefully, twice over. Then, after running headlong into a vigilant pair of grey eyes, he was compelled to look for a small pencil in his pocket, which he fortunately found. He started writing in a thoughtful, important way, looking up to think. He wrote 'A, b, c, d, e, f, g, h, i, j, k, also l. I might even go so far as to say One two three four five six seven eight, the position in which I am in at the moment of speaking is, much as I grieve to say it, deeply as it hurts me to pronounce it, embarassing embarrasing embarrassing is that the correct manner of spelling the word shortly however, hereunder, heretofore some bell or gong will call these people to dinner. Yes, yes yes. Gongs are very good things very likely originating in China, a land where the inhabitants or Chinese as they are called eat eggs so I have been told after they have been soaked in mud for over two hundred years a most peculiar thing.'

Here the gong was heard, and nobody took any notice. Noticeably they did this.

But they were dispersing gradually. Anthony continued his paper on Chinese habits. 'To do under the circumstances under which it was done,' he wrote.

Then he rose, looked at the letter-rack, and strolled into the dining-room.

His table was set for two. He was soon joined by a thin, elderly woman with the most fanciful jumper. They gave a soft 'Good-evening' to each other, and smiled. There followed a bad silence, and alert, curious gazing around the room. This was eased at last by the arrival of their dinner, and smiling mutual assistance to vegetables and salt. 'Be careful, it's hot,' said the woman. 'Oo, it *is* hot, isn't it?' said Anthony. 'Yes.' Laughter and a short silence.

'Have you been staying here for long?' asked Anthony.

'No, I haven't. I only arrived two days ago, really. It seems rather nice, doesn't it?'

'Yes, it does.'

'I've just come back from Germany,' said the woman.

'Oh, have you? It's jolly nice there, isn't it? Things are very cheap there, aren't they?'

The conversation ran from Germany to London, to crowded trains, to Richmond Park, and suddenly to John Masefield, because she had heard him lecture a few days ago. Thence to English Poetry and Literature, of which they had read many works, but a lot of them a good time ago, and they could not quite remember ... Then to Foreign Literature, of which they had read 'Les Miserables' and most of Dumas. (His son wrote, too, didn't he?) They had read Balzac, and Tolstoy, and Turgeneff. Anthony had read some Tchekoff. 'What's he like?' asked the woman. 'Oh, rather gloomy, like all these Russians.'

While consuming the flimsy sweet they came to more personal matters. Anthony explained that he was in London to work for an Exam. She thought that must be a very interesting thing to be doing. Then she roughly outlined her own occupation. Very roughly, and Anthony could not gather exactly what it was. He caught, however, something about 'organising, you know.' That would be right. She looked an organiser.

At last Anthony said, 'Well, I think I really ought to be going. Good-evening.' They both smiled sweetly and bowed, and he went out, and ran boyishly up the stairs, which were wide and flat, lending themselves to this.

He wandered in Kensington till he found a cinema. But there was a queue waiting for all seats. He wandered back, and decided to read 'The Lady from Long Acre' in the hotel lounge, and fall into conversation, perhaps.

But the lounge had no welcome for him. The strong light glared on a blue, pervading mist of smoke. There were some Bridge-players, noiseless, two people reading over the fire, and some children, whom Anthony thought should have been in bed, playing a quiet game of cards, with just an occasional uproar.

He went straight to bed. He was not tired. He kissed the cold stiff sheets, and tried to sleep.

III

There followed many harassing, half-awake thoughts, and thick, whirring dreams, definitely stopped at last by the voices of two men outside, one of whom was taking a bath. The water had ceased to run from the tap, but they still talked. Anthony hoped that this sort of thing would not happen every night.

He lay on his back, thinking. And then he decided to have an orderly Think. He lit a cigarette for it.

An orderly Think was no unusual thing with Anthony. They had begun many years back. Always the Think took place in the softness and nice warmth of bed. There was a set subject for the Think. Many years back, subjects would be '*What I am going to do when I am able to fly with the wings nurse says she is going to get from the poulterer.*' Or, '*What I would do if I was able to make myself invisible.*' Or, '*How I am going to train the white mice given me next birthday to take messages for me.*' Later subjects would be '*My successes in the Brighton and Hove Albion Football Club.*' Or, '*My coming adventurer as the mysterious Hooded Man.*' Or, '*My defeat of Carpentier.*'

But the Think for tonight was of quite a different character. It was called merely '*The Commencement of Life*' For Anthony was going to start Life. Today was Thursday. He was going to start Life on Monday.

It was not turning over a new leaf. It was not just

a greater great resolution. It was starting Life, really and truly.

Anthony had it all lucidly ordered in his mind. He imaged Life, more or less consciously, as a sort of play in three logical Acts and a Prologue. He had just done with the Prologue. The three Acts were (1) fiery youth leaping splendidly to the zenith, (2) replete, mellow middle age, and (3) sedate decay. With a wonderful curtain in Death, bang in the centre of the stage. (You were humorously brave, with delicious witticisms for the grave Doctors. 'For Heaven's sake,' you said, 'keep me alive till I know the winner of the 3.30. I would have died in any case if Lazy Boy's not in the first three.')

At rare times it occurred to Anthony that Life, perhaps, was not quite thus easily dramatic and palpable, but something going less as a smooth, royally rounded curve than as some jagged, thin, sensitive wire, snapped at any insignificant moment . . . But such times were rare. He was going to start Life on Monday.

He had done with the Prologue. That certainly had not been very well played. There had been nothing much to catch hold of in the Prologue. Nevertheless, it had served as an equipment. He was now, he understood, equipped for Life. He was even better equipped for Life than many others, he understood. He had been trained in earliest life by a French governess, an English governess who spoke more French than the French governess, and a German governess who spoke neither English nor German to him.

He had then spent four years at one of the best preparatory schools in Brighton, and four years at one of the very best Public Schools – Westminster. (Certainly it was one of the very best. Eton, Harrow, Westminster, and Winchester, you know ... The Big Four, more or less, really ... A lot of the Cecil family ... Did you ever hear that Westminster once rowed Eton for the right of wearing a pink blazer, and won?)

It had taken eight years getting this equipment, and he could show much for his trouble, having acquired in those eight years truly a host of small arts and accomplishments. And towards the end he had become remarkably proficient at some of them. For example, he could turn English iambics into Latin hexameters, and manage such-like engrossing puzzles, with rare ease, though his translations seldom had quite the same unstilted beauty of the original lines. It was quite enjoyable work. You employed the same ingenuity as in making or solving an acrostic. But it was much better for you than working at acrostics, for you knew that it would be very useful to you, in the long run. Yes, it would be useful, in the long run. Latin was an almost indispensable aid for comprehending your own language. Suppose one day you came across a word like, say, *taciturn,* and you were not quite sure of its meaning – conceivably you might not be quite sure of its meaning – you would remember the Latin word *taciturnus,* meaning silent, and have what you wanted at once. And then it was always very interesting, and helpful too, to note how many English words had direct derivation from the Latin or Greek – '*Stenograph, cessation, ambulation, stethoscope, psychology*'.

Latin and Greek, however, were nothing like the greater part of the equipment given. There were Mathematics, there was Geography, there was some highly specialised History, some playful Science at no odds with a little friendly Bible criticism, and there was English and English Literature. From his earliest years Anthony had been diligently trained in the Glories of English Literature. At first there did not appear to be many of these left over from the works of William Shakespeare, but there were more later. At his preparatory school Anthony learnt that when English Literature was very very good, it was nearly as good as Shakespeare Himself, though of course not quite. Shakespeare's word in Literature, and indeed Life, was wholly as unquestionable as God's word in Exodus, and the devil could quote Shakespeare, as well as Scripture, for his purpose. Shakespeare was an institution, socially interwoven, as the English Church, but was a much sounder institution. For while the authority and authenticity of the latter was in these free-thinking days often challenged, if not flatly refuted, Shakespeare was treated with unflinching faith and piety from all but the most eccentric quarters.

To little bits of English Poetry, however, Anthony took a great fancy, even at his preparatory school. Particularly to 'Horatius' and 'The Burial of Sir John Moore'. Of the latter he gave a fervent recitation in the little dormitory one night, ostensibly for half-scornful motives, but actually with great sincerity and feeling.

At Anthony's two schools, as well as this keen training in the Glories of English Literature, there was plenty of earnest suggestion of the glories of England itself. Old England was glorious, and Anthony was a young Britisher. Shakespeare fully endorsed all this, directly by such plays as Henry the Fifth, and indirectly by being born on St George's Day. At his two schools Anthony's masters had done their utmost quietly to impress upon him that paramount business of a young Britisher – playing Cricket. This was but dimly related to the pleasant summer game. A great mental Cricket it was, an ethic game, seldom discussed. You did not discuss it, but it had to be taken for granted that you were playing it unflinchingly at all times. Whenever Anthony did anything particularly shabby they told him it was 'hardly cricket', and Anthony was deeply ashamed of himself.

At his Public School Anthony became acquainted with a further burden. He was a gentleman. A flexible term, but roughly there were two orders of gentleman allowed. 'Certain something' gentlemen proper, and Nature's gentlemen – a resort granted to those who were plainly not gentlemen. Anthony happily could place himself under the former category. Yet it was undeniably a burden. For it was possible to be a gentleman and yet not be a gentleman. There was a Code ... There were Outsiders, Cads,

Bounders ... If one of these gave offence, to your Women in particular, or even to yourself, you knocked him down. No matter his size. You knocked him down. The matter ended there. Perhaps it was the righteousness of your cause that gave power to your fist.

In spite of the eight years, Anthony's equipment had very little effect upon him. He never thoroughly examined or appraised his equipment. Most vital was the fact that he had it, that from now he was a Public School Man, or an Old Westminster Boy. You went to the best parts of Lords in an Old Westminster tie, and were perhaps accosted by some other Old Westminster. You remembered all your old school slang in a flood, were technically knowing about the cricket, alluded to your People, and gave perfectly sound reasons for not having gone up to Cambridge ...

Otherwise there were very few marks of the equipment. There were still dim notions at the back of Anthony's mind that his studies at Latin and Greek were somehow, some day, going to bear fruit. And in face of a good deal of private and enthusiastic exploration of English Literature, the supremacy of William Shakespeare was never heartily contested by him. It was a case of the Direct Suggestion of an insistent advertisement.

The Prologue he had done with. He began the first act – Youth. This was really the best act of the three.

Anthony had his youth before him as a well-arranged dish, gleaned for the most part from his last year's reading.

It was a selection of the ideas conveyed to him from Compton Mackenzie's 'Sinister Street', Alec Waugh's 'The Loom of Youth', parts of Byron and Swinburne, and the whole works of Rupert Brooke. The latter in particular. For Anthony himself was a small soldier in the great army of young Rupert Brookes – Rupert Brooke having made as many Rupert Brookes as Byron ever made Byrons.

Youth, Anthony was glad to understand, was a phase of glorious ferment, of a wonderful awakening to adventure, to the flesh, the unbelievably sweet elation of love, and the sweeter luxury of love's misery. You discovered early in youth that it was better not to have been born, that life was just around the corner, but you made up for that a good deal by the roses and rapture. The old chant of Beauty was your cry, the passion and the brimming wine.

The above-mentioned writers had clearly suggested his triumphant and melancholy path. Anthony (on Monday) would put a despairing and rosy motto from Baudelaire or some other soft-named French poet on the front page of his youth, as it were, and go consciously and conscientiously ahead with it.

IV

Tonight's Think, however, was not alone 'The Commencement of Life' It might have been called 'The Commencement of Life, and the Coming Months of

Interesting Work and Happiness prior to my Great Success as a Novelist'.

Anthony was not particularly troubled about the Great Novel which would have to figure largely, of course, in the realisation of this Think. Of late he had been pretty sure that he could manage that ...

He had always been pretty sure that he could write. His mother and father, who were both dead, had written. His aunt always said, 'You ought to have it in you.' He had not written very much. When he was younger he had written just the usual short stories. Among these a detective story copied out neatly into an exercise book. It was to have been one of many, because on the front page was '"The Dead Man", and other Stories, by A. C. Forster'. But the only other things that went into that exercise book were two pictures of big liners, and a picture of a goal-keeper making a rare save. This last picture was called 'One minute before time!' The goal-keeper's chin was not too happily executed, and one of his legs was much thicker than the other, and there were pencil splodges around these points – attempts at correction.

And Anthony was very perturbed one night, and wrote the first chapter of a novel, but it was nonsense in the morning.

He took the Vincent prize for English at Westminster, and then there came a short story called 'Retribution', and he had it typed. Everybody said it was very good. Why didn't he have it published?

It was only during his very last year at Westminster that Anthony had definitely decided upon his high calling. It was only after his own private and enthusiastic waking to Literature. The intention had been to be a great Poet (he had two poems taken by the *Poetry Review*), but that did not seem quite practicable, to begin with. For a start he must be a great Novelist.

Again it must not be thought that Anthony was exceedingly well acquainted with this type of literature, to which he was about to make so startling a contribution. He had a one-reading acquaintance with a few of the best-known works of the best-known authors of today, but very little else. When he left school he was still mixing his Samuel Butlers disgracefully.

After leaving school he had a long holiday in Brighton with his aunt. He had planned and thought about the holiday a good deal while at school. It was to have been a holiday of great ease and quiet delight, reading, walking, getting up late, going to bed late, no friends to hate. But when the time came he soon tired of reading, walking, the front, the band, the pier. He was to have fully planned his novel on this holiday, too, but nothing much came of it. One or two ideas came, but there was no systematic planning.

It would possibly be called 'The Splendid Adventure', with reference to youth, and having source in his own experience. An unhappy but vivid ending would be desirable, so as to make it true to life. Also there would be the frequent use of a word often represented in these days by its coy synonym 'sanguinary'. Frequent use. This, too, would serve to make his novel true to life.

And he had the last few lines of his novel already:

He stood for a long while at the window. From below he could hear the hoarse cries of the news-boys rushing down the street. One by one the strange lights of the night peeped forth, dashed with mystery. Somewhere a barrel-organ began to play ......

Or some other words to that effect, inexorably running themselves out in six dots.

And now Anthony had come to Kensington to work with Mr Perring, an Army Coach. He was going to work for the Intermediate Arts Examination.

Anthony had seen to it that his aunt and he should decide that working for that would do him no harm for the present, anyway.

Anthony's Think, in the softness and nice warmth of bed, went something in this way:

'On Monday I commence Life. On that day I go into Life and take a real conscious grip of it. This is not one of my usual resolutions, forgotten or broken in a day. This is *starting Life*.

'On and after Monday I am going to work really hard at Mr Perring's. I will perfect myself in everything he teaches me. Away from school Mathematics, Latin and things will be simply enjoyable.

'I am going to make friends at Mr Perring's, and I am going to make friends at this hotel. I am going to enjoy their most enjoyable companionship.

'My schedule will be regular and enjoyable. I shall be very fit. I shall do physical exercises morning and evening. Ten minutes in the morning, five minutes in the evening. No. Fifteen minutes in the morning, ten minutes in the evening. A cold bath in the morning, too.

'During many of my leisure moments, instead of abandoning myself with the rest to play, I shall study some slightly recondite but improving book, possibly written in a foreign tongue. (My friends at this hotel will observe that I am studying such a book in my leisure moments.)

'But every night, after dinner and with refined ostentation, I shall go upstairs to work at my novel. I shall work all the evening and be a great novelist. I would really rather be a great poet, but novels sell and verse doesn't, so I am reduced to being a great novelist, to make money, to make a name, until I can be a great poet. I shall write at least a chapter every night, full of brilliance, trenchant; a heavy manuscript, typed at last. A book, with coloured, illustrated wrapper, and deep print on thick paper ... Yes, I shall work from seven to ten, regularly. Save, of course, on those evenings when the overwhelming creative mood of the artist renders me forgetful of time. Then I shall work possibly until past three o'clock in the morning. (I shall look very pale the next morning. My friends will doubtless ask me the reason. I may tell them . . .)

'I am going to work in my dressing-gown, and smoke a curved pipe.

'Every week I shall take in *The Spectator*, and *The Saturday Review*.

'I am going to start Life. Hard-working, regular, and delightful. I am going to get a real grip of Life. *I am going to get a real grip of Life.*

'(I shall buy a nice fountain pen for my novel. A really nice fountain pen, an expensive one.)

'On Monday I start Life. Hard-working, regular, and delightful. I have made my rigid schedule and will stick to it.

'(A gold fountain pen in fact. With my initials on it. I will write all my novels and poems with it, and it will last all my life. Thus it is more than likely that my pen is due for some extensive posthumous interest . . .)'

The Think was by now pretty well exhausted. All at once a new Think came. It was called 'The Necessity of Love.'

'I am going to fall in Love,' he thought. 'I can go no longer without realising in some way that swooning ecstasy which I have so well imagined. I am in favour of an exceedingly unhappy love affair, which I throw from me at last, and take to the open road with the friendship of the hills – the sort of love Rupert Brooke so frequently indicated. Yes, I want a very unhappy affair, ending in disaster and desertion on my part. Her sweet face, nevertheless, will be over me as I die. And I shall possibly encounter her, dear as of old, in the Great Dawn . . . '

And the Think began to stray naughtily from the point again.

Anthony imagined that he met the very girl he was wanting at the Fauconberg Hotel. She had beautiful bobbed hair, and was altogether beautiful, let Anthony love her, but returned no affection at all. And one night there was a fire at the Fauconberg Hotel. When it was far too late to do anything, it was found that this girl was still in the burning house, at a window, appealing and terrified.

'I'm going in,' said Anthony.

'It's no good,' said a man. 'It'd only mean two lives instead of one.'

The man fought to hold him back. Anthony knocked him down. (A clean, straight blow, on the point of the chin. The man went down like a skittle. A hard measure, but unavoidable at such stressful moments. The man quite understood. He shook hands afterwards.) Anthony carried the girl out of the flaring house, and then fell, as if dead from the burns he had received.

But the burns did not hurt very much. All about were white, frightened faces. He was lying in the girl's lap. She stroked his forehead and there were kind tears in her eyes. 'I just want you to know,' said Anthony, 'that I have always loved you, and I die loving you – and that's all.' He died in her arms.

Nearly died in her arms, but got well again, was put into a sunny, green room, where the beautiful girl moved gently, and nursed him with pink fingers, and decided to marry him.

Chapter Two

THE NECESSITY OF LOVE

I

The plan was to arrive ten minutes too early, and to walk round about the house of Mr Perring, the Army Coach, who lived in Cromwell Road; then to wait till some boy entered, and follow soon afterwards.

The plan was spoilt because no boy had appeared by one minute to ten. Work was supposed to start at ten. Anthony went to the door and rang the bell. The door was opened by Mr Perring's cook general. Anthony said that Mr Perring was expecting him. The cook said 'Ow, yes, sir', and rubbed her hands on her apron, and looked foolish. Then the door bell rang very loudly indeed, and the cook opened the door for a young man about the size and age of Anthony. He wore white spats and a good blue suit. He had an expression of questioning, serious doubt. He glanced doubtfully at Anthony, and put up his hat and coat, doubting the pegs. Anthony did this too and followed him into a room on their right.

The room had bare boards, maps on the walls, a heavy roll-top desk, a large case full of things which served Mathematics and about seven thickly initialled and engraved, inky, wooden tables, with chairs. A fire burnt fiercely in the grate. The lower parts of the window were covered by fancy green paper, but the light was very good.

'Don't you start at ten here?' asked Anthony.

'Oh, we're supposed to. But nobody ever arrives till about ten past.' Laughter at this.

Mr Perring entered. 'Oh, good-morning, Forster. Did you find your way here all right? Morning, Douglas.' Mr Perring spoke with a deep, resounding, nasal drawl. And his smile was treacle. 'I don't think it's so cold, this morning.'

They all looked into the fire smiling, till Mr Perring broke things with a larger smile and, 'Well – I suppose we must start.'

'Uh-huh,' he sniggered, as apology.

Douglas went to a table, and was soon engrossed. Mr Perring went to a table with Anthony, looked at Anthony's books, and made an amiable exploration of Anthony's existing mathematical knowledge. But he did not get much further with this, because he could not keep from just a quick explaining of some of the things that Anthony did not know. And quite often something went wrong with the quick explanation. Then Mr Perring would, say 'No – that's wrong', to which Anthony would reply, 'Yes, that's wrong.' Mr Perring would work it all out quickly by himself, and give the result to Anthony. 'That's more like it', he would say, and, 'Yes, that's it', Anthony would agree. And so on.

Later two more boys entered hurriedly, each with 'Good-morning, sir. Sorry I'm late.' One of these boys was called St John, and he came from Winchester, and the other was Goring, who came from Malvern.

And later still a small car drew up outside, bringing a young man with the untidy beginnings of a moustache. He came and sat at a table with a paraded quietude and a murmured greeting to Mr Perring. This person was called Cookson, and he came from Harrow. Mr Perring left Anthony and went to the others. Once he left the room. Then there was much excited talk about nothing in particular; a ruler was thrown about the room, and some balls of paper. One of these balls hit Anthony's ear, inter-rupting a bit of particularly arduous work he was on at the moment. 'I'm sorry,' said Douglas. 'Don't mention it,' said Anthony, laughing coyly.

At one o'clock Mr Perring gathered his books and wandered away with a final, diffident 'Good-morning'. Mr Perring always found his final 'Good-morning' very difficult. Sometimes he said 'Good-morning, all', or 'Good-morning, everybody', or 'Well – *good-morning*' instead.

Mr Perring's pupils returned a loud, blatant, easy shout of 'Good-morning, sir!'

They all got up and looked at a new pipe of Douglas's. They were a little restrained because of Anthony, but neglected him. Cookson quietly offered cigarettes to all, without looking at the cigarettes or at anybody. Then he left the room,

'I say, have you seen this pipe?' said St John to Anthony.

'No. By Jove, that's a damn good pipe. Nice straight grain.'

Um-hums and silence.

They were all looking at Anthony, amicably concerned.

'I say, what do you do in the afternoons here?' asked Anthony.

It was all right soon after that. Anthony was able to give his share in an exchange, of limericks that followed – limericks about Young Men hailing from obscure towns, and Points, and Capes, all over the world.

After lunch all except Cookson returned for French. French was a talk, in English, on politics, travel, spiritualism, the nature of God, games, France, with a Monsieur Dupont. Each talker had a pen in his hand and kept before him a French text-book, an exercise book, and some ink. When the talk did not hold him for the moment he scribbled a grubby, ill-considered sentence or two into the exercise book.

On this afternoon the discussion came round to French and English Poetry, and this was good for Anthony. The Frenchman was himself an admirer of Rupert Brooke, and

Anthony had lately read the memoir. He was able to give many details of Brooke's life – the death and dramatic burial.

And then came an exciting moment for Anthony.

'You should meet my sister,' said Goring.

'I should awfully like to,' said Anthony.

'She's awfully keen on Rupert Brooke.'

'Is she really?'

'Yes. She's jolly keen on Keats, too.'

'Is she really?' Anthony was vehement. 'I should love to meet her—'

But at this point Douglas dropped his ink on to the floor, and over his books. There was an uproar, and the engaging turn of the conversation had to be abandoned.

Anthony was hopeful and happy, and his happiness was furthered by learning that Goring lived in Fauconberg Square, only a few doors away from him.

After, he walked to Earl's Court Station with St John.

They talked of cinemas, to which, St John said, he did not go often. He went last week though, and saw Carpentier in 'The Wonder Man'. Anthony had seen that, too. It was jolly good, wasn't it? That fight. Awfully well got up. Good producer, whoever he was. Carpentier not at all a bad actor.

'And that girl in it,' said St John; 'I've forgotten her name. She was topping, wasn't she? Awfully pretty. I didn't think she could act much – but she was awfully sweet.'

'Yes, she was. Did you ever see that film "Intolerance"?'

'No. I didn't. Was it good?'

'Yes. It had some wonderful things in it, but it kept on switching off from one thing to another. You see, there were sort of four themes, and they ran them all simultaneously, and just as you were interested in one they switched off to another.'

'Oh, yes. Beastly.'

'Where do you live?' asked Anthony.

'Oh, right out at Wimbledon.'

'Don't you find it a terrible bore coming up here every day? I'm staying at a sort of hotel place here.'

'Oh, are you? Is it nice? I'm thinking of doing the same thing myself.'

'I wonder you don't. Why not come to this place I'm at. The people are rather weird, but one can keep absolutely apart. We could be together.'

'It would be awfully nice, wouldn't it?. So near old Perring's, too. I think I'll ask my mother.'

'Yes – do.'

They were outside Earl's Court Station. They said 'Well – cheerio', almost in the amiable tones of people who have quarrelled and made peace with tears.

Anthony bought an evening paper and went into the nearest tea-shop. Here he ate crumpets and drank hot tea. A barrel organ clamoured outside, and gave a warm romantic tone to all.

The world really was a genial place, thought Anthony.

Perring did not make you work. St John perhaps would come to the Fauconberg.

And Goring's sister. He went through a lot of indefinite dream business with Goring's sister, the charm fading when the organ man abruptly stopped, and moved away, coughing and spitting.

II

Before getting ahead with his novel of a night Anthony was to wait until he knew for certain whether St John was to come to the Fauconberg. He did not want to be interrupted when he had started. If St John came to the Fauconberg he would wait a week, for politeness to St John (they had spoken of evenings together), and then he would get ahead with his novel.

St John came to the Fauconberg. They had adjoining bedrooms, and they had meals together, and they went into a cinema in Kensington of a night.

They made one or two friends of people in the hotel; a special friend they made of Betty, the pretty girl of twelve, whom Anthony had seen double in an armchair on his first night at the Fauconberg.

There was a great Trouble in Betty's life. This was her homework. 'They really do set too much for the child. She's only twelve,' said her mother. 'Mother's going to speak about it or something,' said Betty. 'She thinks they set too much for a kid of my age.'

St John and Anthony took jealous turns in helping Betty

with it. Once Anthony came out of his turn. 'You know, I shouldn't really be asking you,' said Betty. 'This is Mr Sinjern's day.'

It was an impressive gesture to lie back magnificently familiar and easy with Arithmetic and Lessons, while Betty struggled and said 'Yes', and 'Yes', and 'Oh, yes. *I* see'.

III

One morning Anthony said to Goring: 'I saw a girl in the Square today who I'm sure was your sister. Is your sister tall?'

'Yes – quite.'

'And does she wear a brown I don't know what the stuff's called coat with sort of fur round the neck?'

'Yes, that's right. Hair bobbed?' 'I couldn't see that. She had a red hat.' 'That's right. With a big red feather.' 'That's it. Yes, it must have been her. Funny. I simply knew it was.'

Without result.

Next morning, however, in the middle of work, Anthony's attention was brought to Goring by the latter's energetic windmill signalling behind Mr Perring's back. After attempting for some time to inscribe his message upon the air with a ruler, and being at last damped by Anthony's hopeful, sheepish nods, he put pen to paper and threw a hard little note on to Anthony's table.

'Oh, don't throw notes about at this time, Goring,' said Mr Perring.

Work was resumed with fiery blushes.

'Will you and St John,' said the note, 'come round to my house tonight, and dance? Observe the delicate remains of breakfast suffused o'er Perring's mouth.'

IV

Goring told Anthony and St John to leave their coats in the hall, and took them to the drawing-room on the first floor. Here were Goring's mother and sister, two girl friends of the Gorings, and Cookson. Goring introduced.

Goring's sister was quite pretty enough. She had fair hair, and thin features hardened by pale blue eyes. Her name was Cynthia. Anthony was disappointed. It wasn't really possible. She was like her brother . . .

Coffee was brought, and they talked for twenty minutes. They talked about Christian Science, and none of them thought very much of it. There was a lot of flat jesting about the application of Christian Science to modern straits, getting up on cold mornings, going to the dentist, etc. The originator of it was a Mrs Edwards, or something like that.

'Eddy,' said Cookson. Cookson was on a sofa, hands behind head, cigarette between lips, retaining sufficient power to turn his eyes to those who addressed him.

Inexorably fell the doom of the evening. They were going to dance. And Anthony could not dance. They were going to shift back the furniture and start the gramophone. He said wildly amid the sudden bustling, 'You know, it's terrible, but I can't dance.' But only one girl heard him. 'Oh, can't you?' she said. 'We must teach you.' 'I wish you would.' 'It's quite easy really, you know. You've only just got to keep—' 'Come and do some work, you slacker,' said Goring.

'This chap can't dance,' said the girl. 'Can't you? Oh, you must learn ...' Remarks like 'Strong man wanted here', 'Do you good, old man', and the noise of oiled, moving heaviness prevailed. Cookson spoke to Anthony for the first time. 'Just haul that small chair away, my son,' he said. The gay tune 'Whispering' started. Cookson took Cynthia. (Cynthia was immediately desirable.) St John took the prettier girl. Goring told Anthony to watch his steps and try to learn, and took the plainer girl.

Anthony watched Goring a little, then watched the gramophone and looked at some records.

When the tune finished, he made himself look very doltish indeed by scratching the record in an endeavour to lift the pin.

'Oh, look out!' shrieked Cynthia.

'I'm awfully sorry.'

'No, no harm's done,' said Cynthia, adjusting.

'It's an awful shame you can't dance, Mr Forster. Look here, come and let me show you. Put on a tune, somebody.'

She took him to the middle of the room. 'Now do you know just the ordinary step? This – *one* two three – *one* two three – *one* two three – *one* two three – then turning – *one* two three – *one* two three.'

'Yes, I believe I can do that straight – I don't know about turning.'

'Well – try.'

He tried it straight, but muddled.

'No, you get muddled. Come and try it by my side.' They joined hands and started together. '*One* two three – *one* *two* three – *one* two three,' said Cynthia.

'Now try it properly – with me.'

She showed him how to hold her and they tried. He tripped thrice into her skirt and said, 'It's no good. You mustn't go on wasting time on me.'

'Don't be silly. You'll have to try at first on your own, that's all. Now go all round the room – turning.'

He did this.

Then Cookson, who had been watching all with great care, asked Cynthia to dance.

'All right, just a minute,' said Cynthia; then when Anthony had danced back to her, 'That's splendid. You go on doing that. I'll watch you as I dance.'

Outside, Anthony told St John that it was a lovely night, and suggested a long walk, which was undertaken.

They passed through labyrinths of cold, resounding squares to Knightsbridge, to Hyde Park Corner, then back again. They told stories of their schooldays.

'I believe I could love that girl,' thought Anthony as they talked.

'I am going to love that damn girl,' he said, getting into bed that night.

V

It was not so tremendously difficult. He kept on saying, 'I love her, I love her', and 'She really is exquisite', and he thought a lot about her face and gestures; and he remembered the soft folds of her silk, grey skirt against her silk, grey stockings, and the delicate shoes. He said that it could only be the sweetest-natured girl who would take so much trouble to teach you how to dance. Only a girl, really, of the most guileless and seraphic nature ...

All next morning, to the noise of Mr Perring's nasal drawl, the creaking tables as the sitters changed position, the carts and cars passing, the tradesmen calling in the area, and while the first Spring sun lay, a bright yellow silence, on the road, Anthony meditated upon these things.

He saw her twice during the next week and happily noted a further intensity in his sensations. Sensations varied throughout the day. They were very good in the early morning, just while waking. They were good after meals. They were good when the masked singers, and flute-players, and fiddlers did the song from 'La Boheme' or

'Annie Laurie' in Fauconberg Square. They were not very good with Cynthia, but splendid while undressing the same night. He saw her a third time, and she agreed to go to the National Gallery with him. There would be a walk after that, and he would get ahead with things.

On the National Gallery morning the sky was blue and cloudless. Anthony called for her at a quarter to eleven.

As he waited in the hall, he went through to himself an ordered list of subjects for conversation he had made while dressing. They ran – 'Brighton', 'Evolution', 'Golf', 'Cinemas', 'Oliver Lodge', 'Chess'. The initial letters of these titles taken in this order formed an odd word – Begcoc – odd, but with good mnemonic properties. (It was something like Bangkok.)

Each gave at least ten minutes of talk. 'Brighton' took you to Jews, Lord Allenby, Bournemouth, Eastbourne, and seaside resorts in general. 'Evolution' had innumerable uncharted possibilities. 'Golf' would lead to outdoor and indoor games, 'Cinemas' to film-stars and the sins of Hollywood, 'Oliver Lodge' to Spiritualism and some (conceivably) psychic experiences of his own. 'Chess' to Capablanca and Lasker, and brain.

She came down saying 'I'm awfully sorry I'm late, but I've never been in time for an appointment yet.' Anthony said that *he* was late, and they set out.

'Begcoc' failed him at once. How could he suddenly start talking about Brighton. He said that he had thought it was going to rain earlier in the morning.

'I was probably in my Beauty sleep about that time,' she said.

Laughter. And then, boldly:

'Do you know Brighton at all?'

'Oh, yes, I used to spend a lot of time there at one time ...'

'Brighton' went as far as Earl's Court Station.

'Begcoc' was forgotten. She talked a good deal in the train.

Umbrella and stick were given over at the National Gallery turnstile for '23' on a disc; they climbed the broad stone steps and the agonies of looking at too many pictures commenced. For the first two rooms they were quite happy. At every picture or so they would stop and say 'That's wonderful, isn't it?' or 'I love this, don't you?' and pass on – not without some lack of resolution in determining the exact moment at which they should pass on. Conversation fell into fitful criticism of a more or less fundamental order. 'Exquisite colouring, isn't it?' 'It's not *my* conception of Venus.' 'Who's this by? Lewis? Never heard of him.' 'Wonderfully restful.' 'Yes, you could tell that for a Corot anywhere.' 'Landseer always does animals, doesn't he?' When they had come to the sixth room the close air of the place had made their throats dry, they were weary from much standing, and quite dejected; but like the rest of the dry-throated, weary gazers present they did not even consider capitulation.

When they came out at last the sky was overcast and

attempting snow. The morning was all at once a failure. Love of her was out of the question.

'Thank heaven you brought an umbrella,' he said. 'Shall we struggle to the Corner House or somewhere and get some coffee?'

'Yes – let's.'

They fought the wind up through Leicester Square without a word.

VI

Cynthia, for love, really might have been forgotten. But one evening Anthony gave it out, beyond withdrawal, that he was in love with Cynthia. This was to St John.

It was done in another moonlight walk to Hyde Park Corner. This walk was to have been as successful as the last, but it ended in fatigue, and a prickly heat, and a train from Knightsbridge.

'Have you ever been in love yourself?' asked Anthony at the right time.

'I've thought I have. I don't know if I have really.' St John looked thoughtful. There was a pause, and Anthony waited for it, and it came.

'Have you?'

'No – not really.' He held it. 'As a matter of fact I believe I'm a bit in love now.'

'I can guess who it is.'

'Can you?' Laughter.

'I think I can.'

'Go ahead – guess.'

'I think I can.'

'Well – who is it?'

'Look here, I may be making an awful mistake.'

'It doesn't matter. Go on, old man.'

'Goring's sister.'

'You've got it. What do you think of her?' He was nervous and eager to talk. 'You know, she's really quite pretty, and, I don't know, she attracts me somehow. Don't you think she's jolly nice?'

'Yes, she is. I think she's a jolly nice girl, and pretty too. Do you know, I don't know if I ought to tell you something.'

'What?' Felicitous expectation of he knew not what.

'Well, I'm a bit in love myself.' A very bitter disappointment.

'Oh, yes?'

'With that kid Betty,' said St John.

'Oh, are you? I thought as much. She's awfully nice, too.'

'She is awfully sweet, isn't she?'

'Yes, she is.'

A minute's silence, with a weighty 'Yes' from Anthony.

'Funny thing – being in love,' said Anthony.

'Yes – you just are. You know this kid at the hotel's so frightfully natural. Of course she's frightfully young, and I couldn't admit I'm in love. But when she's older, you know. I think she's so frightfully *natural* and sweet.'

41

'Yes. I think she is.'

'I'm going to take Goring's sister out again on Saturday,' said Anthony.

'Oh, are you?' said St John. 'You'll be able to declare yourself then, won't you?'

'For instance, have you ever noticed the topping way Betty looks worried about her homework?' asked St John.

VII

At this time Anthony saw the first of Diane.

Anthony was balancing himself on the marble edge to the hearth of the lounge fire, just after the sounding of the gong for luncheon.

Diane entered at the door opposite the dining-room. On her way, someone called out 'Hullo, Diane, come back from school?' Diane said 'Yes – rather', and she turned her head and smiled.

For the most part Diane seemed a person who walked quietly by herself. At meals she sat with a clear-eyed and vocationally gentle mother. Anthony said to himself that she was very beautiful in some lights. Like a sort of crushed rose.

Late into the evening she could be found in the lounge, sitting on a red sofa with a young naval man. He talked very earnestly. Diane looked before her, sucked her bead necklace, and listened abstractedly, awaking sometimes to make a light comment.

'Yes. You think you're damned pretty, don't you?' said Anthony to himself, and indeed thought so himself, too.

VIII

There were two copies of *The Poetry Review* with Anthony when he called for Cynthia on the Saturday morning. In these were his two poems.

'I brought two of them that I could find along with me,' he said, a minor poet, already. 'I think they're about the two worst, so you mustn't judge me by them.'

They went by 'bus 31 to Kensington Church. Thence to the Round Pond and the Serpentine. She was most anxious to see the poems, so they sat on green chairs under the trees. The mustard-coloured *Poetry Reviews* were opened at the correct places, and put upon her knee; she read with one arm resting upon her parasol. He leant forward, chin on stick.' I think they're wonderful,' she said. 'I think I like this one best.'

'Do you really? I'm awfully glad.'

'Yes, I do. I think they're absolutely too clever for words.'

'Oh – good.'

A man came and sold them two blue tickets for their seats.

'I say, I'm awfully glad to think you like those verses of mine.'

'Yes – I do – like anything.'

43

'Oh – good.'

'I say, I've got something to tell you.'

'Oh, have you? What's that?'

'Well, let's get up and walk,' said Anthony, with a menace of many things in his voice.

'Right you are.'

Only the sound of their feet on the grass, and her parasol strap clicking. 'Well – go ahead,' said Cynthia.

'Well, look here, I can't just tell it you. Can't you guess it?'

'No – at least I don't think so.'

'Well, if you can't guess it I can't tell you.'

'I can't guess.'

Only the sound of their feet on the grass, and her parasol strap clicking. 'Come on, you must tell me.'

Drama was the way, so he said, quick and low, 'Well, can't you see that I love you beyond all possible words?'

'I thought it was that.'

Now they were enjoying themselves immensely.

'Well, what's to be done?' he said.

'What do you mean?'

Some pathos here. 'Are you going to tell me that you don't want to see me any more?'

'Don't be ridiculous. Why on earth should I? I always did think you were a dear,' said Cynthia.

'By Jove, it's wonderful to hear you say that. You're wonderful.'

'I'm not at all wonderful, and you'll soon find it out.'

'I say, will you let me see an awful lot of you now?'

'Rather.'

'I'm going to cut French out altogether. That'll mean three afternoons in the week. I say, what will your brother think?'

'Oh, he doesn't count. Besides, he's a bit used to it.'

'Have you had many people in love with you, then?'

'One or two.' One has to be frank about these things.

'I must get used to calling you Cynthia, you know. And you certainly can't go on calling me Mr Forster.'

'You're Anthony, aren't you? That's Tony. I shall call you Tony.' She was very much intrigued by the prim way she said, 'I shall call you Tony,' and so was Anthony.

'A nice day, isn't it, Cynthia?' said Anthony. And she said, 'A very nice day, Tony.'

'Do you think you might soon be able to look upon me as your best friend?' asked Anthony.

Grave again. 'You are a very dear friend now.'

They walked along by the Serpentine, and then by the side of Rotten Row talking round and round the thing.

'Of course, you know, I intend to be famous,' said Anthony.

'I'm sure you do.' Not a well-considered reply.

'Those poems I've shown you are just the beginnings. I really intend to do something great.'

'I'm sure you will.' That was better. Anthony held it.

'Are you? You know, I could do anything if I feel you believe in me.'

'Well, I believe in you all right.'

'That's wonderful. You won't be so ashamed of me after all, I can promise you.'

They laughed lightly because she would not be so ashamed of him, after all.

'I suppose it sounds rather cheap,' he went on, 'but I want you as a sort of inspiration. You know, one can't do anything, really, without love.'

'But I'm so very, very empty.'

'You're very, very perfect, and you know it.'

'I don't.'

The lifts were crowded. It was Saturday. He was brought very near to her in the lift. His chin touched her hat.

Cynthia and Anthony were both tired, and a crush in the train with nothing to say was a poor end to their walk.

They emerged at Earl's Court afraid of each other.

'Oh, that book. At the library,' said Anthony. 'They're agitating for it. Could you let me have it?'

'Yes, I'll go in and get it, if you'll wait.'

They let themselves into her house by her silent Yale. He waited in the hall. She ran upstairs lightly. Anthony's legs denied him their customary support. Anthony had decided to kiss Cynthia.

He looked at a Savage Club caricature of her father hanging in the hall.

She came down again. She gave the book to him' He opened it.

'How did you get on with this?' he asked. 'Oh, I thought it was wonderfully amusing.'

'I loved this part about Ram Spudd, the poet, don't you?'

'What's that?' she said, and leant her head over the book. He showed with his little finger.

Edging up to her! Salacious preparations! It wasn't possible.

Yet she seemed expectant. Surely her bearing was expectant.

There followed quite the most unpleasant thing that had ever happened to Anthony, the sort of thing which would make him stop in the street, weeks afterwards, and say 'Oh – oh, dear!'

In his left hand was Stephen Leacock's 'Moonbeams from the Larger Lunacy', in his right hand a walking-stick with an unfortunate crook handle.

He started this Kiss with a dive of the right hand round Cynthia's waist. The left hand made for the lower part of her neck. But 'Moonbeams from the Larger Lunacy' was in this hand. It met Cynthia's shoulder, and dropping from nervous fingers, clattered, all white pages, to the floor. This might have passed. But Anthony made a foolish, small attempt at stopping it, and Cynthia a foolish, less small attempt. And Anthony in the heat of the moment thought it best to get on with his Kiss.

He had not kissed anyone's lips for many years. He had only kissed his aunt's cheeks. And Cynthia's head was in a most unhelpful, wrong position.

It was a Collision. They both tried to get out of it as soon as possible.

'I say – I'm sorry. I hope you don't mind,' said Anthony.

'No – not a bit,' said Cynthia, because she could think of nothing else to say at all.

Anthony had lost his stick. 'Hullo, my stick's got caught in your sash, behind.'

'Oh, dear.'

'Thanks. Well, I suppose I must be going.'

He opened the door.

'See you again soon,' he said. 'Good-bye.'

'Good-bye.'

She closed the door the faintest bit too quickly.

Anthony stood quite still, at the bottom of the steps, for a quarter of a minute, and looked at the pavement.

Chapter Three

DIANE

I

Anthony never saw Cynthia again. He meant to see her again. He told St John that he had had rather a row with Cynthia. St John was sympathetic and helpful. Their tactful ingenuity gave birth to a Cousin whom Anthony was always having to visit of an evening. 'Remember me to your sister,' said Anthony to Goring. 'And tell her I'm hoping to see her as soon as I can possibly wangle it.'

II

Anthony had a letter from his aunt. It was a faded letter, written in pencil. She was very unwell, and in bed, she said. 'I wish I could be up and about to enjoy the beautiful weather I can see from my window,' she wrote. 'I suppose it will be *raining* when I *am* well.' There were instructions about Spring clothes, and the danger of them in the variable Spring weather, and there were worries about damp hotel sheets.

III

Shortly after Anthony was disillusioned.

Disillusionment at Anthony's time of life is ever the most delightful and proud experience. Later, people find that they are losing their disillusions, which is good, of course, but not so good as losing illusions.

It started with Anthony, really, while he was walking home alone in Kensington one night.

He had a light headache. He lit a cigarette and inhaled, deep into his lungs. The smoke, breathed out through nose and mouth, and knowledge that it came from the chest, gave a delightful sense of manly dissipation. He narrowed his eyes, thrust out his jaw, and did it again and again.

He lit another cigarette from the old one, and decided to smoke more cigarettes in the future. Cigarettes, really, gave a better tone than a pipe, if you inhaled them.

The wind was cold, the muddy pavement shone here and there under a flickering lamp. The public-houses were closed, dark, and chill. An old man with a fine white beard played a fiddle jauntily in the street.

'God. Damn funny thing, life,' said Anthony.

Then he saw another old man talking in low tones to a painted woman.

That crowned it! He was disillusioned after that.

He was overwhelmed by the thrilling sordidness of it all!

He gave the hollow laugh of sophistication and was deeply, calmly happy.

He passed a woman hastening along with her little boy. The child trotted by her side, babbling pluckily in spite of the hurry.

'The innocent child . . . ' said Anthony, very gravely.

'The innocent child . . . Huh!'

Disillusionment ran riot for a week. Anthony knew too much about everything to be enthusiastic about anything. So he kept a great calm. He aided his speech by few gestures. His hands were in his pockets. He was tired. He went to bed late. He sat deep in armchairs, and with Cookson, moved only his eyes to answer those who spoke to him. He called all men, old or young, 'Old Boy' – unconsciously thus denoting his sense of morose kinship with his fellow-voyagers in this forlorn journey of life. Once he called an old lady an old boy.

He inhaled his cigarettes, he bought a bow-tie and a sports-coat, and grey flannel trousers, wore them together and brushed his hair neatly. He encouraged the blue rings under his eyes.

But the disillusionment phase did not run riot for much

more than a week, being exorcised eventually by the sports-coat, which was all for an athletic phase, and had its way. For this the bow-tie succumbed to an Old Westminster tie, and a blue collar came in, with a neat tie-pin. Shoes became brogue, and socks dull green. And bed came early, and cold baths came. Cigarettes gave way to pipe, and smoking was done once after meals only. Which condition did not conduce to the long life of the phase.

For the first three mornings physical exercises were taken before breakfast. The pyjama coat was doffed and Anthony stood in front of the glass unable to resist an unrestrained admiration of his own bust. The human body was really rather a beautiful thing . . . He would then have imaginary, but formal boxing-matches (heavy-weight) with a ghostly opponent far bigger than himself. Things looked poorly for him at the opening of these bouts, but *lay* tremendous skill in about the fifth round he would out-box and knock out his large opponent (who, by the way, had been ostentatiously confident of success). Then he dressed, feeling very weak, but certain that exercise like this must be doing him a lot of good.

One Saturday afternoon, he thought it would be a good thing to go and watch some cricket, sit in the sun all day and get nicely browned.

He went to the Oval. He took a train to Victoria, and thence by deep-rumbling tram to the Oval.

Out of the noise of the tram, through the noisy turn-stiles, into the wrapped silence of the ground, broken only by the scrunching of his feet on the gravel, and the distant cry of 'Card – card . . .'

The ground was packed. This irritated Anthony, not so much because there wasn't a seat for him, but because he had thought it would be rather a good idea to go and see some cricket, and here were all these people who had had the same good idea, and they weren't taking any notice of him . . .

The match was Surrey *v.* Middlesex.

He looked at the score-board: 115 for 9.

Middlesex were batting. Anthony looked at the field. He picked out Hobbs at cover. He picked Sandham, who turned out later to be Peach. He picked out Fender, a giant, genial note of interrogation in the slips, and he found Hitch.

He seated himself upon a warm stone slab. Happy laughter rose as Hitch quaintly took an easy catch from Murrell.

The Surrey eleven were immediately chased helter-skelter into the pavilion by small autograph-hunters, and Anthony waited for the people in the front seats to get up and go home to lunch, but they didn't.

Later, however, he was able to force himself into a doubtful place in the front row. On his right side was an old man with a beard – the inquiring type of old man who picks things up in the street. On his left was a young boy with a green school cap.

Out came the umpires, unable to cope with a sense of their own importance, and receiving ironical applause.

Then Hobbs and Sandham. Hobbs played brightly for some minutes, but was soon out leg before wicket. In the next three-quarters of-an hour Sandham went, followed soon by Shepherd. Peach and Ducat made a long, tiresome stand.

The heat became oppressive. Anthony was wondering, for no reason at all, where the old man with the beard lived. The old man was not unlike W. G. Grace. Anthony wondered whether the old man with the beard had ever thought himself not unlike W. G. Grace, or whether he had wondered whether anybody else had ever thought him like W. G. Grace ... Which Anthony was doing ...

Devilishly hot. The old man made a silly remark about the cricket.

Ducat was caught in the long-field, and the sun faintly relented. Fender came in and started things with a six. It was a pleasing summer's day with a nice breeze. Fender hit a four, was nearly stumped, and hit a four. And another. He played back to the last ball of the over.

A maiden over at the other end with Peach. Joyous expectancy for Fender, who hits a three. The whole ground and Anthony very happy.

''Ere's a bit of cricket,' said the old man with the beard. 'This is what we call a cricketer. 'Ere's a bit of cricket.'

Anthony looked round the ground. He noticed a young man walking round the great restless circle in his direction. An untidy young man with a cap too large for him, slouching and looking about.

He looked to Anthony like the junior attendant at the hotel . . . The young man walked in front of the screen, was hidden by a fielder, and moved away at his leisure.

The old man with the beard made a silly remark about him.

Fender hit another four . . .

Was that young man looking for him?

When he passed Anthony would not notice him. He would look in front of him and not notice him.

Another six from Fender. Deafening applause. The young man, fifteen yards away, made a sign to Anthony amid the noise. The noise faded to nothing. Silence itself was deafening as Peach played.

The young man said loudly to Anthony, 'I'se told I'd find you 'ere, sir. I brought this telegram, sir.'

Anthony blushed to fire. He looked at both sides of the telegram. 'Oh – thanks.'

The young man made to go away. 'I'll see you later, I suppose,' said Anthony. The young man went away. Anthony put the telegram into his pocket, and watched the game. He could sense the old man with the beard edging further away from him, so as to get a better view of him. He could hear the old man's heavier breathing owing to the strain of this. Fender was bowled. There was a whoop and a thunderous roar, and Anthony stood up, and walked away.

He did not know what he was doing, or where he was going at all. He was wondering if his aunt had died. He noticed that the crowd were not looking at him. He noticed a young boy, all covered with yellow, dried grass on which he had been lying, throwing an apple-skin at another young boy ...

He went behind the stands. He was alone for a moment and undid the telegram, fumbling. *'Aunt much weaker glad to have you here tomorrow Fletcher'*

Fletcher? Who was Fletcher? That must be the hotel proprietor.

'Tomorrow.' It could be nothing very bad. Certainly it could be nothing very bad. He wished, though, to take a train to Brighton at once.

But it wasn't urgent.

He felt very low. He thought of drinking something, and then thought of watching the cricket again. It might take his mind off; but his seat would have gone, and Fender was out, and it wouldn't take his mind off. He did not know what to do.

He saw Hobbs in a blue blazer, coming out of the Players' door.

He went unknowingly through the turnstiles. He waited while two trams, full up, refused him, but found a place on the third. The tram rumbled through the crowded, littered streets. A very cheerful man was sitting in front of Anthony, and kept leaning back and talking to a cheerful girl and her mother. They went over Vauxhall Bridge. The Thames was filthy.

*

He met St John off the steps of the Fauconberg. He told him at once. 'I say, I'm awfully sorry, old man,' said St John. 'But I think everything must be all right as the telegram says tomorrow.' They talked round and round the matter for some time. The conclusion was that everything must be all right.

At last Anthony said, 'Well, I suppose I ought to try and throw it off my mind. What are you doing tonight?'

'Well, as a matter of fact, I'd arranged to go to a dance with Betty,' said St John, uncertainly.

'Oh – good.'

They went into dinner soon afterwards. The food was so much nasty substance wrongly in Anthony's mouth. He did not know what to do. There was nothing to take his mind off. He would not be able to sleep tonight. 'It's no good – I must get out of here,' he said to St John:

'Right you are. I'll come with you.'

Running hard upstairs was a relief.

'You get into bed', said St John, when they were in Anthony's room, 'and I'll read to you or something, till you get really tired, shall I?'

'But you're going to dance with Betty.'

'No – I'll go and tell her about it.'

'No – rot. As a matter of fact, I hate being read to. I don't mean that, but you know, I hate being read to, as a matter of fact. I'd far rather settle down here, with my pipe and a nice book.'

'Well, have you got a decent book?' St John looked at the table. '"Intentions" – Oscar Wilde.'

'I really want something rather light,' said Anthony. 'Can you lend me anything?'

'Afraid I can't. I'll tell you what, though. I'll run in on a bike to Kensington Library and get this changed for you.'

'No – I can't trouble you, old man.'

'Not a bit of trouble. I'll run in now. What book would you like?'

'Let's see. I want something very light. I know. What about "Tarzan of the Apes"?'

'Suppose it's not in?'

'Oh, get anything you choose.' Anthony was speaking in jerks. 'No, I know. I'd like a Dickens. One I haven't read. "Martin Chuzzlewit." Or "Dombey and Son." "Tarzan", "Martin Chuzzlewit", "Dombey and Son." Or any one you choose. Thanks so much. Oh, and one thing more, old man. You might get some chocolate or something while you're out. About six bars of Cadbury's nut milk. I'll give you the money.'

St John said 'Rot,' and went.

Trembling a little, Anthony undressed, put on his dressing-gown, and stuffed his pipe. St John returned, wonderfully quickly, with 'Martin Chuzzlewit' and six bars of Cadbury's milk chocolate. He couldn't get the nut milk.

He asked Anthony if there was anything more he could do, and left him.

Anthony adjusted himself to his pillows, took the first bite of his chocolate, and opened 'Martin Chuzzlewit'.

He ate his first three bars of chocolate with zest, the

fourth without zest, the fifth dutifully, and the last with disgust. Then he lit his pipe.

He didn't enjoy his pipe. It was not good after chocolate. All the time he was trying to read 'Martin Chuzzlewit'.

A wind was coming. The blind was flapping against the window. Outside the door was heavy silence.

He read, *'But here again the sneering detractors who weave such miserable figments from their malicious brains are stricken dumb by evidence'* He didn't know what it meant. And he was not attending to it. He was looking over the top of his book, listening to the blind flapping.

'But here again the sneering detractors who weave such miserable figments ...'

Some women and men were laughing heartily downstairs. Of course, it was a dance night,

'But here again the sneering detractors who weave such miserable figments from their malicious ...' Somebody had turned the water on in the bath. Its trickle became louder and hollow as the water rose ...

'—dumb by evidence ...'

'But here again the sneering detractors who weave such miserable figments ...'

There was girls' laughter, and rushing outside. Betty whirled in followed by another little girl. 'Hullo,' said Betty, 'I thought Mr St John might be in here. He's vanished into thin air. We're playing 'hide and seek'.''

Evidently Betty had not been informed.

'All right, don't go,' said Anthony.

But Betty had gone, half-closing the door,

Anthony heard vehement, earnest whispering outside. Betty was heard saying, 'Cumm onn! Don't be sillee!' There was a scuffle and Diane was dragged into Anthony's life, looking very foolish, and saying, 'How do you do? I don't know *why* Betty insists on my coming in here.'

'Have you been playing "hide and seek" or something?' asked Anthony.

'You've got a new dressing-gown,' said Betty.

'It's not new,' said Anthony.

'Isn't she in*sult*ing?' said Diane.

'Won't you sit down and talk?' said Anthony.

Betty flung herself stormily on to the bed. The other little girl followed. Diane was in black satin evening dress, with a thick woolly coat over it. This coat was a green sort of dark-blue colour. She kept her clenched hands in the pockets of this, as though she were cold. She sat in the armchair with slow grace, and then sat sweetly upright, hands still in pockets, smiling.

'I don't know why we're all sitting here like this,' she said.

'Oh, shutt upp, Diane!' said Betty. 'Hullo, do you play chess?' She went over to Anthony's chessmen.

'Yes – rather.' Then to Diane, 'Do you?' 'No – I don't. I wish I did. But you have to be terribly brainy to play chess.'

'No, you needn't really be a bit brainy. I'm not brainy, anyway, and I love it. I must teach you one day.' 'I wish you would.'

'Come on,' said Betty. 'Let's play chess. Can four people

play, Mr Forster?' 'Yes, I suppose they could if they tried.' Betty brought the table to the centre of the room, and spilt some of the chessmen on to the board, and some on to the floor. Diane helped to pick them up, and then brought her armchair to the table, and sat in it sedately, and watched.

Anthony gave the names of some of the pieces and said where they should go.

Diane took a pawn suddenly and looked at it and at Anthony. 'I know what these little ones are called,' she said, and looked at the ceiling. 'Don't tell me.'

'Oh, I know, Mr Forster, I know!' said Betty. 'Oh, Mr Forster, I know! Let me tell you!'

'No, let her guess,' said Anthony. Diane looked at the floor, smiling.

'Oh, you are a fooo-o-l, Diane! I know, Mr Forster! Let me tell you, *Mister Forster!*'

'Pawns,' said Diane.

'I say, shall I teach you how to play chess?' said Anthony to Diane.

'Yes – do. I'd love it.'

'Oh, well – if you're going to play *chess* – we're going.' Both little girls went noisily out of the room.

'This is where we're compromised or something, isn't it?' asked Anthony.

'I say, shall we light the fire. It'd make it more cheerful. Don't you think so?' said Anthony.

'Yes. Don't trouble. I'll light it.' She took the matches from the mantelpiece and bent over the fire.

Anthony wondered at the white marvel of her neck, and the thick hair, bobbed. And he noticed the smallest, crumpled, pink handkerchief in the gaping pocket of her woollen coat.

He began to teach her how to play chess. She knew how to move the knight. 'It goes all squiggly.'

'I know,' she said. 'It goes one straight one squiggly.' She moved the knight round the board as it should go. 'One straight one squiggly, one straight one squiggly, one straight one squiggly, one straight one squiggly.'

After Anthony had been teaching some time, after Diane had been overwhelmingly penetrating and far-seeing (for a beginner) and forgotten things sometimes, but always saved herself after looking at the ceiling, they found they were tired of this, and had cigarettes.

'I'm awfully glad you came here tonight. I've been feeling absolutely beastly and miserable this evening.'

Diane had already curled herself in the wicker armchair, playing with a castle. Now she came quickly upright again, and looked at Anthony.

'No – why?'

Anthony looked awkward and funny, and an awkward, bright light came into his eyes.

'Oh – I dunno. I've had an absolutely beastly telegram saying my aunt's awfully ill.'

'Oh, is she bad?' asked Diane, in the most French and sudden way, and she put her hand out on to Anthony's hand.

'Well – I don't know. Shall I show you the telegram?'

62

'Yes – do.' She read the telegram quickly.

'Oh, it couldn't be anything *rea-ea-lly* serious. Because if it was they'd have told you to come tonight. Oh, I'm sure it's all right.'

'I suppose it is,' said Anthony.

'I hope it is,' said Anthony.

'Oh, I'm sure it is,' said Diane, absolutely sure.

There did not seem to be anything more to be said about it. Diane was playing with her castle again, putting a highly polished nail between the crevices at the top of it.

'You see, it's so rotten, because my aunt's about the only person who's alive.'

'Why, haven't you got a father or a mother?' asked Diane, almost angrily.

'No, you see, that's why it's so rotten.'

There was silence, and really nothing more to say, now. Diane tried to say 'What a shame!' softly, but Anthony ran into it with, 'Anyway, let's change the subject. I ought to try and get it off my mind.'

They started to talk, and it was not long before they fell to talking about love. She was going to leave him at eleven. Eleven came very soon. She was going to leave him at a quarter past, twenty past. Then it was happily decided that she should stay till twelve. Her mother didn't count. Besides, she would never know.

Diane had a lot of little complete stories about love to tell. Stories about herself. They began with, 'Oh, I must tell you', or, 'Oh, it was so funny', they continued very rapidly, wandering quickly up a side-path sometimes, reached no climax at all, and ended with a quiet 'Ri*dic*ulous', or 'Funny', or '*Chee-ee-k*'.

There was, most often, a young man in them who adopted an attitude or merely uttered something which should be crushed, and she had crushed it in the best way. The feeling about it was that it was all his fault, anyway, for being in love.

Diane's premise was, basically, that being in love was all rot. Anthony thought so too, really. At the same time there were some really Big Loves, and love could absolutely make or mar a man's life. Diane was to look at Keats and Fanny Brawne. There was a difference between being in love and Loving. Anthony had, as a matter of fact, been 'in love' only a little while ago. But he had seen the folly of it.

'I'm going to wait now,' he said, 'till I can find real love.'

'Yes, there must be such a thing,' said Diane.

Here they found each other's eyes.

Really Anthony might have looked through the myriad coming preliminaries and said, 'I love you, Diane. It is real love. I am not "in love" with you. I love you.' But he said, 'I don't know if one'll ever find it.'

It was five to twelve now. Diane had replaced her castle, and was scribbling stiff, black star-fishes on the first sheet of the writing tablet Anthony had bought for making notes about his novel.

64

'You know,' said Anthony, 'I've got an awful sort of feeling that I don't know how I'm going to get through to-night. I wish I could buck up and get to Brighton. It's the suspense that's so beastly.'

'Yes, it's the *suspense* that always is. But I know it's all right, really.'

'I'll stay with you a little longer if you like,' said Diane, softy, while scribbling.

'I say, you're awfully sweet, but it's got to be gone through with. So we might as well go through with it.'

'You must cheer *up*,' said Diane. Then she wrote on the writing tablet. 'You must cheer UP because there's nothing to be WORRIED ABOU—' But the point of the pencil broke on the emphatic U. 'Well, I suppose I must go. Good-night, then.'

'Good-night.'

They didn't know whether they should shake hands, and it ended by Anthony shaking two of Diane's fingers.

She went out, closing the door softly.

Anthony knelt and put out the noisy gas fire. The hollow shouting abruptly stopped, and the red asbestos faded to chilly grey. He switched off the light and got into bed.

He felt that he would sleep. 'I'm not going to think,' he said aloud. He was warm and comfortable. The hotel was in deep silence, the deeper by contrast with the long even flow of talk which had just finished.

There were quaint night noises and creakings on the stairs . . .

Soon Anthony's mind was rushing headlong through a thousand inconsequent images. Sleep was coming.

It was not long before Anthony became too hot. Then the obsession came. He kept throwing off his clothes and trying to forget the obsession. The obsession was something about a purse, which should have been black, but was always being grey. It should have been black. All was uneasy if it was not black, and good and comfortable if it was.

Later, Anthony began mixing tar with some soft yellow cheese. That made a fizzing noise, and swarms of grey beetles were born. It was a chemical formation. Formation. Why had it not been discovered before? Funny thing that tar had never been mixed with yellow cheese in the whole history of the world. The history of the world. Perhaps Pythagoras had discovered it, but let no one into the secret ... Here Sir Oliver Lodge put in an appearance, and felicitated Anthony upon his discovery. 'Shakespeare would have done no better,' said Sir Oliver. Anthony wondered what Shakespeare had to do with the matter, exactly. The beetles were getting much bigger, dangerously bigger. Sir Oliver Lodge was nodding, and quickly becoming King George. 'We must let nobody know,' said Anthony to his Majesty.

And again, '*We must let nobody know!*'

He woke, and found the words ringing through the room, all grey with the bright light of the full moon.

He sat up, stiffly and suddenly, and looked at the moon, and shivered.

He leant over and tore away the sheet of paper on which Diane had been scribbling, and looked at it for a considerable time.

The stiff, black star-fishes glittered in the moonlight, and he could distinguish the words about cheering up very well.

There was something soothing and sweet in the stiff, black star-fishes in the light of the moon, and in the meaning of the words, and in all the funny, emphatic sweeps of Diane's young hand ...

Anyway, he was kissing the paper soon, and turning in bed, and drawing it as near to his heart as he could.

Chapter Four

THE DANCE

I

Being pleasant is certainly one of the most important luxuries of unpleasant people. (A man is supposed to hate his benefactor. He does not do this so much as simply not change his opinion of him.) Everybody, pleasant and unpleasant, had been very kind, and wonderful, and good to Anthony after the death of his aunt.

Eight weeks later he stood on Brighton Station, holding a heavy suit-case, and bound for Kensington again.

He asked a porter the number of his platform, and was undeniably wounded because the porter told him the number of his platform with no particular soft adaptation of his voice; though it was admitted that the man could not possibly have known.

All down the platform there were little clusters of people outside the carriages seeing other people off, and finding nothing to talk about. He found a third-class carriage with a corner seat for him.

A train came in on adjacent rails, and Anthony played the game of imagining that his own train was moving. Then he played the game of F with the advertisements in the carriage.

'Doctor Collif Browne.'
'Haftingf and Ft Leonardf.'
'When Knightf were bold
They all wore armour.
Nightf hot or cold,
Wear Fwan Pyjama.'

The last did not adapt itself well. He tried another game which had occupied him a good deal lately – the game of turning upside down, or reading backwards.

Doctor Collis Browne was good – 'Enworb Silloc Rotcod'. And Swan Pyjama – 'Amajyp Naws'.

Something said that the train was about to start. The seers-off said 'Well—' and held out a hand or a cheek, and five minutes later the train moved out – clanking quietly.

It was a yellow, drizzling day. Anthony found a comfortable position and lit a cigarette. He breathed it deep into his lungs.

Anthony felt that he was about to start a completely new life. It was Wednesday. He was going to start a new life on

69

Monday. He was going, on that day, into the world and he was going to take a real grip of it. In his suit-case were letters of introduction to different editors, sub-editors, art editors, and secretaries of many of London's leading newspapers and periodicals. These were written by a Mr Jarrold Wemyss, who had been an old friend of Anthony's father, and who was seeing to Anthony now. These letters were brief, saying that Anthony was 'a good lad, very keen, and should be most useful to train, etc.', that he was a nephew of the late Sir Charteris Forster, that he didn't mind where he started.

Mr Wemyss had taken it quite stonily for granted that Anthony was going to work tremendously hard and not mind where he started. Anthony did not like this presumption of Mr Wemyss very much. As a matter of fact he had intended, all privately, to work tremendously hard; and here was Mr Wemyss expecting nothing else.

Anthony now had three pounds ten shillings a week of his own. This was to be sent to him every week. When he was twenty-one, he understood, he was to have quite a decent amount of money. Not enough to marry on, but quite a decent amount of money.

Anthony was quite sure, really, that he would be successful in obtaining a very good journalistic position. Also he had a certain fear in the obtaining of a good journalistic position. Wemyss had frightened him with stories of frantic interviewing, reporting, and putting papers to bed. There seemed in journalism a quite unfamous, distressfully energetic note of competition. Not that Anthony did not relish a bitter fight for fame. But he did not like this way of setting about it. A far nicer way of doing it would be to starve somewhere, in a garret, writing immortal things, and being free. Even being found dead one morning in the red, new sunlight ...

The train began to go very fast, bawling under bridges. Anthony looked at the advertisement of Dr Collis Browne. He pictured Dr Collis Browne as an agreeable and patronising man, very affable with the nurses beneath him. Anthony had had some experience of nurses and doctors, lately.

For no reason the name 'Fuller Maitland' leapt into his brain ... He wondered who Fuller Maitland was. He had seen his name somewhere. It would be rather a good thing to put into a novel. A man who suddenly thought, for no reason, of the name 'Fuller Maitland'. At a critical moment ... He found another comfortable position and began to doze ...

At Croydon he was well awake and depressed.

At Victoria he dragged his suit-case to the buffet, and he ordered Bovril. He drank this at a copper-covered little table. He looked all the time at one of the barmaids, who was just too fat.

When he reached Fauconberg Square it was raining venomously. Fauconberg Square was smaller than when he had left it.

The hotel had been repainted. The door was slightly ajar. He walked into the lounge. A new-lit fire spluttered largely in the grate. The hotel attendant came out.

'Hullo,' said Anthony.

'Ullow, sir.'

A pause. 'Well, I've come back.'

'Ow, yes, sir,' said the attendant, musingly. He might have been saying, 'Well, well, we all have to come back – in the end.' Actually it was tenderness for the death of the young man's aunt.

'How are all the people getting on here?' asked Anthony.

'Oh, jusser same ye knowsir.'

'St John's left, hasn't he?'

'Ow, yessir.'

'Yes. I had a letter from him. Is that girl,' said Anthony. 'You know – the girl who's father's French, and her mother. Are they still staying here?'

'Ow, now. They've gone away, sir.'

'Oh?'

'B'lieve they're comin' back in a few days though,' said the hotel attendant, and walked away to get on with his work.

II

Anthony was having the cold lunch in the cold dining-room, three days later, and Diane and her mother arrived, wearing their hats. He watched Diane and smiled at her once. Her mother looked at him.

After lunch all the people gathered round the fire. The rain poured down outside. A milk-cart stood by the pavement. One could hear the milkman's tread on the stone steps down below. The people talked about 'Monsieur Beaucaire', and about Valentino, and Novarro, and Moreno, and Novello, but they couldn't see what other people saw in them at all. And they talked of playing cards. The children talked of playing hide and seek and thought they were going to have a very enjoyable afternoon. Anthony talked to Diane. He brought out a pipe, and drew the smoke into his mouth as hard as he could, emitting thick clouds. This was to convey to Diane a certain manliness, a certain manly need of tobacco, unsatisfied by normal smoking. Diane's mother was still looking at him. Nothing ever was said about Anthony's aunt.

'Do you dance?' asked Diane.

'Yes – a bit,' said Anthony.

'Coming to the dance tonight?'

'*Is* there one?'

'Rather. There's a sort of Club that holds its dances here. And lots of people from the Fauconberg go.'

'I should love to go. You're going?'

'Oh, yes.'

'Will you dance with me a bit?'

'Rather.'

Silence, and nonchalant peering out of the window.

'What are you doing this afternoon?' asked Anthony.

'Oh, I've arranged to go to a cinema with mother.'

Shortly after he left the hotel and went to a cinema in town, and forgot about Diane.

73

III

Anthony felt his cheeks, smooth after shaving. He struggled and adjusted his shirt and collar, and tied a successful black bow. He looked in the glass many times, under the reddish light which was always kind. He slipped on his dinner jacket. He ran into a disconcerting side-view of himself in the glass, and re-brushed his hair to combat it.

He was quite nervous. Tonight would be his first proper dance. He was frightened about his own dancing, about the laws of dancing. He didn't know how he was going to ask anyone to dance with him. He would be rather a nuisance to Diane.

Just before going into the dining-room he met Betty. He told her to ask her mother if she could come to the dance. Permission was given and Anthony felt safer. You could make Betty dance with you, and it would be all to the good, with Betty, if you did badly.

After dinner Diane made things very difficult by going through a door and not coming back. He stood for a long while in front of the lounge fire and told some nearby acquaintances that this was his first proper dance. They were comforting. They told him that there was nothing to be nervous about, with dancing as it is done now, anyway.

The lounge became nearly empty. Bridge was being played at two tables. A newcomer read a book timidly in a corner.

Suddenly Anthony thought they might be dancing

upstairs. He ran up the stairs, and through some half-dark passages. Music, hushed, came to his ears. Then he came to the ball-room.

There was a great noise and dazzling light. The ball-room was very crowded. The tune was *'Ma, he's making eyes at me!'*

The colours were really beautiful. The music was invigorating. It set the eyes alight. The girls' dresses were beautiful, short, with clean, sweet lines. All about was adorable pink and heavenly light blue. There was a satin mauve dress. One girl danced in pure white. The men were in gay, black evening dress.

Some old women with elaborate grey hair and heavily beaded frocks sat in the room and watched. Outside, by the door, two plain girls spoke cheerfully and exhaustively about normal matters to a very good-looking young man. On the stairs were stray couples going indefinitely up into the darkness, with a tendency to giggle the more, the higher they went.

It was the suburban triumph. The dancing and the band were suburban. The girls were suburban. Their beautiful dresses were suburban. The men, too. They did not look like men in evening clothes, but like men wearing evening clothes, save the ultra-handsome few, who were far too supreme . . .

'Ma, he's making eyes at me!' It burst out so loud and measured that you knew it would soon end.

Anthony saw Diane dancing.

Diane was indeed beautiful. She was not the usual sweet-mouthed, clear-skinned girl of her age, who eats chocolates, smokes a little, goes to the theatres without a hat and in an astounding cloak, is sympathetic, plays the piano badly and Chopin's 'Marche Funebre' incessantly, loves her mother, dances well – who bites, and tugs, and rolls her small pink handkerchief, and infuriates a host of boys with an abandoned longing for her flesh. Diane really did walk by herself.

She had bobbed hair. It was thick and profuse, nearly startling, but not startling. Its colour was uninteresting. Her body was slender, alertly, almost primly upright. Her hands, her feet, her shoulders were exact in perfection. Sweet was the word for her face. Neither pretty nor beautiful, though you might have said that it was, like a Shelley lyric, so intensely sweet as to be beautiful. Her eyes were light brown, of an almond shape, and all tolerance. Her skin was lovely as it could only be at her age, which was seventeen. Her nose was small and her mouth was too big, and maddeningly passive. A natural pout and droop at each corner, and so a softly melancholy demeanour when her eyes did nothing.

On this night she wore a red silken dress, thin, short, and simply arranged.

Anthony said, 'By God, she is rather beautiful,' and he was made happy by the music.

The music gave its final grunts, softly enough to make noisy the regular shuffle of feet. The music stopped. The dancers remained poised for two seconds – then they broke away. The partners who did not know each other well looked foolish and said 'Thank you' to each other, and clapped. Some moved to the door. The clapping went on for about seven seconds. A pause. One large clap, followed by a few little claps. Then there was nothing but talking.

People were looking at the stranger Anthony as they came out. He thought of Diane only. She was standing in one corner of the room looking funnily in front of her while a side-whiskered, dark, South American sort of young man sheathed in a blue suit spoke to her. Once she laughed, looked up at him, and looked in front of her again. A disturbing sight for Anthony ...

Then she saw Anthony, waved a hand at him, said something through smiles to the man (who bowed and smiled), and came towards Anthony.

'Hullo-o,' she said. 'I'm so glad you've come. I thought you were lost.'

'Oh, no, I'm not lost. As a matter of fact I didn't know they were dancing. Where did you get to?'

'Oh, I went to change.'

'Oh.' Laughter.

'First-rate room this, isn't it?'

'Yes, it is. Good floor too.'

'Is that so? I suppose the floor makes a lot of difference, doesn't it?'

'Oh, yes.'

'Of course, I suppose unless the floor's good one must

naturally get terribly tired . . . ' And so on, bravely, battling the pauses.

The band started. He asked her to dance. They set off. The room was a wonderful, bright kaleidoscope again. Diane was strange to Anthony's touch. Her hand, poised out with his, was cold, and slid from his hand. She was looking brightly and nonchalantly at the other dancers. Her smooth face was very beautiful and young. There would really be no joy in kissing that face of hers. Perhaps a tender, fatherly joy.

'What is your name, by the way?'

'Diane – de – Mesgrigny,' she said, mock deliberately. 'I absolutely hate it.'

'No, it's jolly nice.'

'Oh, it's not. What is your name?' This last with a strong flavour of her accent. She asked the question without the questioner's tone, as another might have said 'There is the man.'

'Anthony – Charteris – Forster,' said Anthony, mock deliberately.

'That's a frightfully ripping name.'

'Oh, it's not.' It was a very happy dance. After it she was lost. She was found later dancing with the South American man. But she smiled at Anthony and he felt that the evening was his.

Then came the supper interval. They all went down for refreshments, laughing. There was a great crush in getting lemonades and ices. The girl in the satin mauve dress dominated the scene, and obtained the required honey-pot effect by sitting on the floor, tailor fashion, and pretending to beg for her ice, and by laughing louder than anyone else. Anthony was with a Woman. He looked with a dull, nervous longing at Diane, who was at a small table listening to a young Swede of the Fauconberg.

What a listener was Diane!

In spite of the noisy mauve girl she was plainly the attraction of the evening. Yet she was being most attentive to Anthony. He was quietly proud.

The band started again, and soon the dancing. After about half an hour he managed to be with her alone, at the door. She said, 'I've an awful shoe that's hurting me.' He felt very tender about her hurt foot. Then he said, pluckily, 'Come downstairs and have some lemonade, or coffee, or something.'

'But I've just had some lemonade.'

'Never mind. Have another.'

'Right you are.'

The lights had been half turned down in the dining-room. She sat at a table and he brought two lemonades. They talked about theatres, and Matheson Lang. She simply loved the things he was in. They talked about Mr Bottomley ... It was simply terrible, she thought, after all those luxuries, champagne, etc., to be put in prison. They supposed he was an absolute rogue, though. Did the poor people out of money.

Then they found that they were perhaps distantly

related. Anthony had had an uncle who had married a Frenchwoman called . . . She would ask mother about it . . .

All the time he was looking hard at her face. Her mouth was too big. He didn't think that other men could see the charm which he could see, which, of course, would make it easier . . .

They agreed to go and dance. She said 'Thanks awfully' for the lemonade, and wanted it to be put down on her mother's bill. He said, 'Don't insult me.'

Going up the stairs he put out an impulsive, friendly arm behind her, touching her other arm, and he withdrew it before she had really noticed it.

They came in time for the last dance. It was a selection of popular tunes.

Anthony danced with Diane. He was taken with a vague, thrilling excitement. He held her a little firmer. What a sweet, coloured thing she was!

A dear satisfaction swept over him as he held her, and left him excited, eager to recapture it.

He was starting life afresh on Monday. Life was hardly difficult enough for him. But, yes, it would be a terrible battle; a coloured, sunset battle . . .

He held Diane a little closer still. He would like to hold her in the darkness, in the grey and red dawn, she weeping, he to fight the world . . . How sweet to die for this purity in his arms.

The dance ended. The band played 'God Save the King'. Anthony felt foolish and nearly stood at attention. All the other men stood very firmly at attention. They had, manifestly, been in the army.

Diane was somehow swept away from him in the talkative exodus. He waited eagerly for her 'Good-night', which came with quite a special smile for him.

In tremendous spirits he ran downstairs, past some sly jokers who were putting on their clothes, into the smoke-ridden lounge, where the Bridge-players sat, and had sat through it all. He pitied them.

He went and looked at the cold, grey ashes of the big fire. He was happy and not thinking about anything. He noticed that one piece of ash was quite brown, instead of grey.

Chapter Five

STARTING LIFE

I

When Diane had reached her room after the dance, and shut the door, and played with her hair and looked at it in front of the glass, and made a small red place on her face redder by rubbing, and stared at her face blankly for some time until she was frightened, and started to undress, she thought a good deal about Anthony.

She liked Anthony very much. She liked his evening clothes, and his name, and his eyes, and the death of his aunt; and she hoped that he would soon make love to her.

Diane's lovers, past and present, were almost countless now. Nevertheless they were often counted by Diane.

Diane was still at school – an expensive school in Hampshire, kept by nuns. All the lovers wrote to her at school. In the cupboard of her room was an old, big hand-bag crammed to bursting point with letters. She had had fifteen lovers. Sixteen if you counted in her cousin. They were taken for the most part from the Fauconberg during her holidays. Only two remained. The rest were now but subjects for some highly interesting and also a little spiteful speculation. She expected they had married. Got hold of some little fool or other, she said.

Of course Diane doubted if she would ever really love. She had even once made an earnest stipulation to that effect. That was after the affair with Jimmy. Jimmy had been wonderful. Dear Jimmy. When she had been unkind he used to show a neat little revolver, or wouldn't eat, or talk, or he would sit in the lounge all night, thinking. He had the name 'Margot' tattooed across his chest. He was supposed to be receiving imploring letters from Margot. That was why Diane was unkind to him. She felt for Margot. She nearly wept for Margot, and Jimmy, and herself.

The Margot business, the danger of dying by his own hand, and because he was the first with her, made Jimmy stand out well from the rest. She kept a photo of him in a silver frame, to which she often said 'Dear old Jimmy,' and often, in the dusk, she had kissed it.

There were Dick Montefiore and Douglas Baskomb. And there was her cousin, who had kissed her – but he was her cousin ... And during them all was Jacques. Later he gave the most trouble to Anthony. He had known her for five years. He was twenty-six. He was very friendly with her family, and came from a good French family. Anthony knew him for a detestable and dishonest person, with a mind grown thick with a fifth-rate order of sentiment, which he exhaled at all times with Diane. He was tenderly angry with Diane when she told lies. He took cigarettes out of her mouth in a funny, charming way. He had thrilling ideas about 'jeune fille'. One day he kissed Diane – cleanly, gravely, openly. The kiss reeked of 'future little housewife'. He had chosen his 'little partner through life'. And after that he kissed Diane whenever he had the opportunity, which was often, for he liked Diane's lips, and he did it in public.

Diane loved Wallace Reid. But he died.

At the present time Diane was particularly interested in old men of about forty-five, a little bald, and very, very wealthy ... She was probably going to marry one of these and be petted by him.

She had a quick, bright mind making as fast as it could for shallowness. She took a proud satisfaction in applauding those curiously 'precious' little sophistications scattered throughout the pages of 'The Smart Set'. Paradox all for the sake of paradox, and epigram for the sake of epigram. She had just made a wonderful epigram of her own. 'All men,' she had written to her best girl friend, 'are fools; but I tolerate them because they are dancing fools.' (Diane was a splendid dancer, by the way.) She had a certain noble ideal about men, though, because in her copy of 'Esmond', on the page where Beatrix resorts to tears, she had written 'Men – real men – *hate* tears.'

Alec was her very latest lover. This was the naval man. She was trying out new things on Alec. She was being cold, without heart, heart-breaking, beautiful and inapproachable, relenting at times to give ecstasy. Alec had entreated a good deal, and then had lost his last chance with Diane by acknowledging her new attitude. He had called her a 'little iceberg. 'She was a 'little iceberg' from then. Alec was getting a bit tired.

'Of course,' Diane would say to herself. 'What I really want is a man who would thoroughly take me in hand ... ' She very much liked saying that ...

II

It was Monday morning. The Monday starting Anthony's life. He had been walking up and down for some time outside the offices of *The Daily Post,* wondering which was the right entrance, and waiting until it was quite ten past eleven.

All about were dirty carts filled with packages. Refuse was everywhere. The buildings were high and the streets narrow, shutting out a bright, sunny day. *The Daily Post* was written in many places, so was its companion evening paper. To Anthony the whole effect was inimical, preoccupied, not wanting him at all.

He chose an entrance and walked in, pushing a door which said 'Pull'. A thickly-medalled attendant looked at him.

'Could I see Mr Sladen?' said Anthony. 'I was told I could see him if I called between eleven and twelve. I have a letter here.'

'Yes, sir. Would you wait in here, sir?'

'Oh, thanks very much.' That was friendly enough.

The attendant took him along a passage into a small room with one chair and a copy of *The Field* on a table.

Anthony expected to be kept waiting a long while. He sat down and tried to read bits of *The Field*.

The attendant put his head round the door.

'Will you come this way, sir?'

'Oh – yes.'

He followed the attendant along the passage again, and up some wide stone stairs surrounding a lift. The attendant knocked at a large neat door. There was a distant murmur from within, and Anthony was shown in, and left alone with Mr Sladen.

The room was all neatness and cleanliness, like the offices in the advertisements for Young Men of Ambition, who are seen convincing their directors. On the desk were many loose papers. Behind the desk sat Mr Sladen, in sober grey.

'Ah, good-morning, Mr Forster,' he said, stood up, gave his hand to Anthony, and ushered him towards a chair in a manner altogether dental. 'I received a letter from Mr

Wemyss, and I thought you'd be calling.' He opened and shut drawers. 'Now where *is* that letter?'

Anthony thought Mr Sladen a wonderfully kind and nice man. 'Do sit down,' said Mr Sladen, still opening and shutting.

'Ah, here it is.' He put the letter in front of him on the desk, and leant back in his chair, put both elbows on the arms of his chair, made his two second fingers meet on a level with his collar, and looked across at Anthony. His eyes were as grey and sober as his suit.

'Let's see. How old are you?'

'I'll be nineteen next March.' He was to have said 'Sir', but it didn't come well after March.

'That's only eighteen then, really?'

'Yes-er.'

'I suppose you haven't had any experience of this sort?'

'No, sir. I haven't.' Abruptly. (You can see, can't you, I'm a frank and businesslike young man.)

'But this sort of thing has always been my ambition. I'm frightfully energetic and keen to learn.' (The sort of young man you want, I believe.)

'Have you any knowledge of French or Spanish?'

'Er – French. Yes, French. Quite well. Very well, really.' (Don't you start testing me!)

'Of course it needs a little polishing up,' Anthony murmured. (Don't you start testing me!)

'Any shorthand or typewriting?'

'No. No shorthand. But typewriting . . . a little . . .'

'Well—' began Mr Sladen, and talked so kindly to Anthony during the next ten minutes that Anthony thought him the nicest person in the whole of the world. He had nothing to offer Anthony. Nevertheless he gave his advice to a young man starting out in life. Anthony was to try to get on to a provincial paper where he (Anthony) did and learnt everything. After ten minutes Mr Sladen got up and wandered to the door, talking, and opened the door for Anthony. Anthony said 'Thank you very much' far too many times. Mr Sladen said, 'Good-morning,' and gave his hand. Anthony took the hand and said, 'Good-morning, sir.' And then, 'Thank you very much, sir,' to which Mr Sladen did not reply. And Anthony stumbled, all stick and gloves, out of the door.

Anthony ran down the stairs with a weight off his mind – and body it seemed. He said, 'Good-morning' to the attendant, and went into the warm sun and brisk wind. Very, very elated.

'Of course,' he said, 'I'll have to go to someone else to-morrow, but I won't be nearly so nervous now. Anyway I have the whole day in front of me.'

His legs were taking him nowhere.

'I'll have lunch in town, and then I'll go to a show.'

'I'll go and have a drink,' he said. He went into the saloon of the nearest public-house. It was ill-lit by daylight. There was the soft murmur of men's voices, and the noise of levers jerking, the ring and clatter of the till. He ordered a double whisky, and took it without the offered water. The first sip was very bitter – then fine warmth inside him. The rest of the sips were bitter and nasty.

III

But on the Tuesday morning Anthony met Diane in the lounge and fell to talking with her. 'Well, I really must be going,' he kept on saying. 'Oh, must you?' said Diane. 'I know,' said Anthony. 'Shall I put it off for tomorrow? I easily can, really.'

Diane sat on a red sofa, and he on the arm of it, and they remained like this all the morning. They had a long talk right up to the sounding of the gong for lunch. During their talk people from the hotel went out for walks and came in again tired; and people from the hotel came and talked with them. Diane and Anthony took each other's side in every argument. If they disagreed they soon found they had misunderstood each other's exact meaning. He had his arm along the back of the red sofa, and when she leant back he stroked her hair with his forefinger.

In the evening a game of hide and seek was arranged by Betty and another. This was Betty's joy. To select carefully a few companions, to make her camp on the half-lit stairs, to make war upon, elaborately conspire against, and utterly scorn all the staid, unknowing people downstairs, until her mother trapped her at last, for bed. Anthony and Diane played on this evening.

'Hide and seek' was soon dropped because the hiders ran away when they were near to being found, and so were never found, and the seekers did not really like being seekers; so the games of 'Knock at Mrs Steele's door and run quickly away and choke with suppressed laughter' and 'Climb up the Fire Escape'. and 'Dress up as Ghost' were tried. And all the time Anthony was coming into suppressed laughing contact with Diane, and touching her cold hands, and her hair, as she whispered.

And with Diane, hand in hand, he undertook the most exciting expedition of the whole evening. That was to go down the darkest passage and see if it really was a dead man lying on the trunk (privately rather believing in him, and hoping).

And nearly every night, after games and things, Diane and Anthony found themselves alone by the grey, old fire of the quiet lounge. They spoke about Love generally, with the usual sudden irrelevant excursions and short stories from Diane. Anthony gave his ideals on these matters. He insisted on the difference between being 'in love' and Loving. All the people who had been in love with Diane had been 'in love', he declared.

And when Anthony was in his room after these long talks, and thought of Diane moving about in her room, only two doors away, he wondered how he was going to tell Diane that he loved her.

There seemed two ways at the moment. One might

happen next Saturday, during the dance. While they were sitting on the stairs he would say, 'Oh, I can't go on with this any longer.' 'What do you mean?' 'Oh, *you* know what I mean.' 'I don't.' 'Oh, yes, you do – can't you *see?*' Then it would be easy.

Or ask her into the billiard-room the day before she went back to school, in three weeks' time. 'Look here, I've got something to say to you which I simply must say before you go away. I love you. No – don't say anything, I want to talk to you for five minutes on end . . .' Then it would be easy.

But one night it came quite simply, and not according to plan.

Diane had just said, suddenly, 'You know, it's a funny thing, but I feel I can make anybody like me if I try long enough.'

'When you say "like", do you mean "love"?' Very grave.

'No, Anthony, of course not.'

'I suppose it's rather hard for a man not to fall in love with you.'

Confusion.

'Oh, rot,' said Diane, softly.

'At least that's what I find,' said Anthony, almost inaudibly.

'Oh, rot,' said Diane, quite inaudibly.

'But you must remember I'm not in love. I Love.'

'Do you Love now, then?'

'Of course.'

'Who is she?'

'You, of course.'

'Meee! Oh, it's so silly!'

Here the Swede came up. 'Ar! Yoo too, torkeeng as ushool!'

They spoke very happily to the Swede.

The next few weeks were certainly the happiest for Anthony with Diane. They went for walks together, they went to the dances together, and they sat together every night in front of the grey, old fire of the quiet lounge.

Directly they were alone they consciously skirted about awhile on small matters till a chance remark let them talk of Love, and then they never left it.

Diane was supposed to like him very much – better even than Jacques. He was her Best Friend. He was 'waiting for her'. One day, it was hoped, she would 'come to him'. Diane quite thought she would do this, too ...

They were always being 'hurt' by one another. Diane was the great one for being hurt.

They built happily a thousand sentimental difficulties and positions for themselves, and forgot them straightway.

One night Anthony was taken out by the Swede, and given some whisky, and this intoxicated the young man – not seriously, but his eyes became a trifle steadier than they should have been. Diane saw him in this condition. Next morning Diane said to him, timidly:

'You mustn't do that again.'

'No, I know I mustn't. And if you say so I won't.'

'I do say so.'

'Well, I'll never go near whisky again.'

Anthony was an inured toper and Diane was his angel. What influence these women have!

Anthony had decided to wait until Diane returned to school before seeing any more editors or people – until he had received his first letter from her.

IV

Sample of talk between Diane and Anthony by the grey, old fire of the quiet lounge:

'And you know, Anthony,' Diane says, and has to give a little gasp and a swallow because she has been talking so quickly, 'you know once an absolutely terrible thing happened to me because of that. You see, down at Nunton I and my friend Rosalie (Rosalie and I, I should say), you see, we used to go blackberrying, and so as to get through brambles etsettrer and not get torn, we used to take off our skirts.'

'Oh, yes.'

'Well, once we were doing this, you see. I'll absolutely never forget it. We were just by the railway embankment, and suddenly a terribly good-looking chap came round the corner.'

'No need to drag in about being good-looking.'

'Well – he *was*. Anyway, I absolutely shreeked and dodged behind Rosalie, you see. She'd got more on than me, anyway. As a matter of fact, Anthony, I'm not a bit ashamed of being seen like that. You know, Anthony, when I get to my room every night and take off my things (petticoats and things), I'm absolutely terribly proud. I wouldn't mind *who* saw me. Look here, Anthony, why *is* one supposed to be ashamed?'

'Oh, Diane, you are a scream.'

'I'm not, Anthony. That's what everybody says about that. Oh – I never told you about Mrs Mackintosh, did I? You know, that awful woman who used to stay here? How she started lecturing me for passing her and her son's room just *once with* not many clothes on when I was going to get some water from the bath?'

'No – you never told me.'

'Ye-e-s, rather; she came into me in the billiard-room. You know how she talks – "Wah, wah, wah, wah, wah, my dear child, you may think that this sort of licence is all right for France or wherever you come from, but it certainly won't do heah, war, war, war, war, war, war, war, you may think you're very clever and attractive, war, war, war, war, war," and so on like that. So I didn't say a word all the time. I kept quite calm, And when she'd finished I said, "My dea-ea-ea-ear Missiz Mackintosh, I shall inform you when I wish to receive your advice as concerns my future gui-i-dance. Gui-i-dance. Gui-i-dance!"'

'Guidance.'

'Guid-i-ance?'

'*GI*dance!'

'*Gi*dance. *Gi*dance. *Gi*dance. You know, Anthony, I can't speak English nearly as well as I used to since I've been to France this last time.' Diane nearly has to swallow things again here. 'And I said – "I most certainly don't want that advice now." So she went stamping out of the room in a fewerus rage, wah, wah, wah, wah, wah!'

Sudden deep silence. A reader in a corner of the lounge copes with his large newspaper, making a quiet rattling noise.

'Chee-ee-eek!' says Diane meditatively, looking at the fire.

'Yes. I suppose it is rather ...' says Anthony, looking at Diane.

Prolonged silence.

'Of course, Diane, it doesn't really matter your going about dressed like that. But you know lots of men would rather like to see you like that. That's where my love's different, you see, Diane.'

'Yes.'

Silence.

'Oh, Diane, I do love you terribly.'

'Yes, I know, Anthony.'

And another silence.

'Tell us about the good-looking young man. I suppose he asked you to marry him after a little while, didn't he?'

'Oh, yes, I'd forgotten,' says Diane, waking up again. 'He was terribly nice about it. Just as though nothing had happened. He asked me and Rosalie to go back to tea with him. Needless to *say* we didn't go. I believe Rosalie would have, though – oh, Anthony, you really ought to meet Rosalie.'

'I don't want to meet Rosalie a bit.'

'Oh, why not, Anthony? She's terribly pretty, and I really believe you'd fall in love with her.'

'Oh, Diane, don't say ridiculous things like that. It hurts me. It shows you couldn't understand my love for you a bit.'

'All right. I'm sorry. But, Anthony, she really is sweet. And she's got a terrific sense of humour. I must show you her last letter to me. By the way, she says she's met this chap in London ...'

V

'I say, Diane, will you give me a photograph?'

'Well, as a matter of fact I haven't got a proper photograph. But when I get down to Nunton I can send some snapshots.'

The last afternoon. They walked down Regent Street together. That night she left for school. Anthony was excited, and nervous, and happy – happy, too, that she was going. Letters from her with a vague scent, and all in her funny, sweeping handwriting. Snapshots of her, in open places, or with trees behind. And sweetest joy of all, letters *to* her! Time to think out dear, telling things.

And the music and warmth of the crowded restaurant where they had a comforting tea made Diane very tender.

She became rasher with kind words for Anthony every minute. And when they came out it was as though quite a new friendship had come upon them – an intimacy that had never been.

They walked down Haymarket, into St James's Park, thence to Buckingham Palace. Crossing by the immense erection of Queen Victoria surrounded by her white, bloated magnificence, Diane took Anthony's arm. The supposed motive was protection against a passing taxi – but she didn't withdraw it.

It was all as happy as a happy dream for Anthony. With Diane's arm in his, however, he was conscious of a difficulty in carrying his body. If he held himself too upright there came an irritating association with pillbox hatted soldiers seen rigidly 'walking out' in old-fashioned prints. And if he let his shoulders slack, he felt that his shoulders were slack. When she took her hand away with a murmured 'There', he was sorry but easier.

The train was crowded and they had nothing to say. At Earl's Court he was very nervous and wanted to get done with the farewell.

'You'll write to me once a week, won't you, Diane?'

'Yes, I promise you I will.'

'Nice long letters?'

'Rather. And you will write to me?'

'Oh, I'll write every other day.'

They came to the steps of the Fauconberg. They went up the steps and she turned, and held out her hand.

'Well – good-bye, Anthony.'

This was not at all right. He had had his own ideas about the farewell. He was to have begun it himself, and kissed her hand at the end, perhaps. He took her hand slowly.

'Well, is this the last I'm going to see of you?' he said.

'Yes, you see, I've got to go and pack things now.' She was looking down at their hands. He withdrew his.

'Well, you will write to me, won't you?'

'Oh, *rather*, Anthony.'

'Really long letters?'

'Yes, and you mustn't forget to write to me.'

'I can't see myself forgetting.'

'Good-bye,' he said, ran down the steps and walked, looking right in front of him.

He went into the garden of the Square. He walked up and down the grass, which was a deep glowing green in the sudden fresh peace of the evening. The evening sun caught the trees, making them rich unearthliness – a mass of twinkling golden coins. A gramophone grated a tune which he could not follow, from an open window. And there was a dim rumble from the traffic in Earl's Court Road, lost in the angry uproar of a 'bus as it passed.

Anthony wanted to cry. That is to say, he wanted to have the desire to cry. He had no desire to cry.

Directly he heard from Diane he must set about looking for a job. And he must get on with the novel.

He would look for a job every morning. He would

spend his early evening writing to her – then late into the night with the novel. A thick manuscript, typed at last. A book with coloured, illustrated wrapper and deep print on thick paper.

He was going to start life on the Monday after the day he heard from Diane. He was going to make himself money and fame, and he was going to marry Diane. And all this had to be done as quickly as possible. His novel was the thing. He must work hard at that. On the whole it would be better if he failed to get a job ... But if he did get a job, he would work at the novel as well, if he had to spend the whole of every night at it.

This was not to be the usual kind of resolution, forgotten or broken in a day. The position was made for him. Diane and the whole of life were in it.

In front of him, as he worked, there would be a snapshot of Diane among trees.

In this evening sun there was a sweet colour and sadness over the future.

A taxi came moaning from the distant rumble of the traffic, and drew up outside the Fauconberg. The hotel attendant came out with the baggage. Diane and her mother came out. She kissed her mother, and her mother left her. Diane stood for a moment in the last, red glory of the sun, looking about her. Then she went inside the taxi, and the taxi, with a quiet air, took her away.

Anthony was despairing for a moment. It might have been the smart travelling frock of Diane. She seemed far too beautiful, and out of his reach.

He felt that he must write to her at once – an immediate counter-move.

He walked quickly to the post office. He asked for a letter-card. In the semi-darkness, and quick bustle and thudding, feeling nervously elated as though it were the red eve of great adventure, he wrote this:

DEAREST DIANE,

My only excuse for writing this note is complete misery.

I don't know how I'm going to get through these first days. Think of me as much as you can, Diane dearest,

Yours ever,

ANTHONY.

He walked back along the Earl's Court Road, which in the twilight seemed much quieter than usual.

Chapter Six

THE NOVELIST

I

The next day was given to writing a letter to her.

He wrote a rough first draft, and corrected, and copied neatly. The aim was to avoid crudity, or repetition, or schoolboyishness. He had to find the matured way of saying 'Oh, Diane, I do love you so.'

On the day after next he had a letter from her. He came downstairs with a leaping heart and looked at the rack. There was a whole bundle in the F portion. There were two type-written letters to Mrs Franklyn, and then a blue rich-papered envelope addressed to him.

He took it quickly and put it into his breast-pocket, and walked towards the window. There was no one else in the lounge. He took it out and felt it. Very thick. He tore it open, fumbling. A lot of loose blue pages pencil-written on each side. He glanced at the first.

'Dear Anthony,' he read, 'I was very hurt at seeing you last night and that you didn't come up and say good-bye to me. You know how I wanted you to . . .'

'This is going to be wonderful,' said Anthony, and put it all straight into his pocket, and went into breakfast.

After breakfast he settled in an armchair, and read.

DEAR ANTHONY,

I was very hurt at seeing you last night and that you didn't come up and say good-bye to me. You know how I wanted you to.

Oh, Anthony dear, I'm feeling so unhappy and wretched. I arrived at this mean little station of Nunton, with its funny little mean buildings, so different from London so tall so noble so lofty.

('She is very young,' thought Anthony.)

Anthony, I feel as though I want somebody to take me away from all this. I don't know what it is, but I feel that I could sit on my bed and cry and cry and cry. I've received your tiny note and I can't tell you how it relieved me. Anthony, I give you permission, I WANT you to write to me *whenever* and *however* you like. And I'm longing for your next letter, so there.

Like this for nearly four more pages, all with the same flavour of pouted lips. Then a white line.

Thank goodness, I've received your letter at last. Anthony dear, I can't tell you how glad I feel for all you say. And I only hope that one day I shall be able to reward you for your kindness and nobility, and well, love, Anthony dear.

I enclose a snapshot of little me, and I know it's hideous and I don't care, so there, I've got a better one somewhere and I'll try to find it and send it by my next letter. Etc.

Anthony did not quite know what to feel when he had finished this. He was at least tremendously grateful for a most unexpected affection on her part. The 'Anthony dears' were heaven. But he had to acknowledge that the letter was just the letter of a schoolgirl feeling normally downcast and romantic on her first night at school. And she certainly was very young.

He did not love her very much for the next few days. Diane had been far too kind to him.

He changed his attitude. She should not be Laura and Egeria . . . She should be a beautiful, innocent child, to be caressed and adored beyond her understanding.

But this did not last after her second letter. Diane pulled round after a week at Nunton. She was, without quite telling herself so, feeling quite disgraced by her first letter to Anthony. And she observed, without quite telling herself so, one or two vague presumptions and liberties in Anthony's response. She set about to recover the old state of affairs, without making the transition too apparent.

But she did feel most kindly towards Anthony, and her second letter was as long as the first. The implication was, however, that Nunton wasn't such a bad place after all. And it dwelt a good deal upon the tennis she was playing. And it neglected quite a few of Anthony's questions about Love. And it remarked, in an off-hand way, that a letter had been received from Jacques, who had just gone out to South Africa. It quoted Jacques at some length. And the last page was very hurriedly scribbled and said they were waiting for her to go and play tennis.

His letter after this second letter was all surrender and appeal. The old circumstances were in again, and Diane began to give Anthony the very worst of Diane.

Diane had a 'style'. The most common method with her was the *London Mail* method. A short, pithy sentence, and a line drawn quickly across the page. Sometimes the next sentence would cap the last. And instead of underlining often you would find very large capital letters.

Extracts from fourth and fifth letters:

Anthony, do you play?
_____

TENNIS of course.
_____

I think tennis is the loveliest thing in the world. It's nearly as good as dancing.

And LOTS Better!!

When I get back to London I'm going to play ALL DAY LONG. I'm going to play with that chap Dickson from the Fauconberg, who, by the way, I've heard from, and another friend of mine and you if you like.

And the other friend of mine *isn't* a MAN.

So don't get JEALOUS!!!

I note that you write your questions out in tabulated form so I proceed to answer them in the same manner.

1. Question. Do I imagine that I have ever been in love?

Answer. No. I might, Anthony, have given my love once to our friend B, if he had been what I thought he was. You see, Anthony, I am *very, very* affectionate, but much more, oh, ever so much more proud. And I am very, very cold. Hence I have been called a 'little iceberg' and a few other things like that by one of my 'friends'.

2. Question. Do I think I will ever love *anybody*?

'Answer. I don't know. It's just possible.

But I don't think I shall ever really love anybody who is in love with me.

3. Question. Do I realise that your love for me is the greatest I have ever had?

Answer. Yes, Anthony dear, I think that your regard for little me is the greatest I have ever received. Tho' I can't think why. What can you see in me? I really haven't got one decent feature. *Look* at me.

Eyes and nose bad
Hair frightful
Mouth awful
Figure middling
Feet and ankles bad
Complexion all right
INTELLIGENCE VERY NORMAL.

Anthony accepted this without inward comment, as some lovers of religion will absorb the irrelevant vagaries of a creed.

II

Anthony waited until he received the proper snapshot of Diane before looking for jobs and getting on with his novel.

But the snapshot did come, and Anthony spent a dreadful

week of mornings. He would climb up the stairs, or go up by the lift in terror, have a hasty interview, and come down the stairs again, very happy. Nobody had anything to offer him. He was to try to get on to a provincial paper.

Anthony was to have worked at his novel on the evenings of these mornings, but that was given up. Writing to Diane took most of the rest of the day.

But one Monday evening Anthony started his novel.

III

On this Monday, after tea, he strolled into the Earl's Court Road and bought a thick exercise book, costing a shilling and sixpence, a pen, some relief nibs, and two double B pencils.

After dinner he went to his room, switched on the light, lowered the blind, took off his coat, put on his dressing-gown, lit his pipe, ruffled his hair, got out the small wicker table, put the ink and writing materials upon it, adjusted his legs in it, opened at the first page and started thinking, about himself, in a dressing-gown, with a pipe, about to write a novel. The romantically complete novelist.

Then he began to think about his novel.

Beyond the fact that it was, in face of a vivid and calamitous ending, to reveal from his own experience the ardent splendours of Youth's adventure, he didn't quite know what his novel was going to be about.

He would probably spend tonight making notes, perhaps sketching the first chapter.

He must devote this first evening simply to planning the thing.

He disentangled legs from wicker table, and tried pacing up and down the room. At last he wrote on the first page of his exercise book, at the top, 'The Splendid Adventure,' and tried some more pacing.

Then he saw that he'd forgotten to buy blotting paper. He would write in pencil tonight. But in the future he would always write in ink. That might be one of his idiosyncrasies as a novelist. He could never write in pencil. ('A relief nib,' he would say to an interviewer, 'bluish ink, some poisonous shag in an old pipe, and an exercise book for one shilling and sixpence.')

Then he put a note of interrogation, in brackets, after 'The Splendid Adventure'. Then more leonine pacing for three minutes.

He wanted a plot. He wanted a plot. Now what was that idea he had a few days ago? ...

Suddenly he closed his fist and jerked it in front of him.

'I have it, I have it!' he said. 'Jove, there's a great joy in creating!' He hurriedly entangled his legs, and hurriedly scrawled underneath his title:

Girl and Man Love
  Splendid A.
All beautiful. Describe

Girl gets money. Spoils. Traitor to Splen Ad

He poor. Vanishes.

One Eve Fancy dress ball

She there. He turns up dressed as beggar

Says fancy really real dress. Marvellous scene. One
night of joy stunt. Pathos.

She says going marry. He goes out into night.

She relents. Remembers S.A. Goes to his room

Irony fate. God's jest. Finds him dead. Killed himself.

Final scene description of him on floor. Blood. Barrel
Org playi ragtime tu outSIDE.

Anthony was very happy after this, and walked about
the room for some time, thinking about its goodness, and
filling another pipe ...

('It was written,' he might say to the interviewer, 'in a
small room at the top of a small hotel in Kensington, with
the not infrequent interruption of various gentlemen of the
hotel taking their baths. It is a bad book. I can only hope that
by the writing of it I have fitted myself for something better.')

Then Anthony decided to find the actual circumstances
and scene of his story, and this he found more difficult.
What was the Occupation of his two characters, and
what their standing in life? Did it take place in London?
Or Brighton?

'This wants a lot of thought,' Anthony thought. 'One
can't decide all of a sudden.' On the whole it would be best
to brood on it.

Yes, he would go down now, and try to get some billiards. And he would brood on it.

The next evening he went to his room with the shad-
owy presence of reluctance. And when he had put on his
dressing-gown, and entangled his legs, and lit his pipe, he
wished that his pipe was curved. He could work better with
a curved pipe.

He tore away last night's page ('I ought to get a note-
book,' he said) and wrote 'Chapter One' at the top of the
next page. Then he thought that he must do at least one
chapter this evening, and as the first would be short, he
might get well on to the second.

In five minutes he was writing:

Madge put down the book she was reading, and began
to feel the sensation of dreariness which always inevita-
bly comes towards the end of a train-journey.

A soldier opposite chatted to a parson. A woman did
her best to control her two ugly little boys who seemed
anxious to run into Madge's legs.

Croydon was a long way ~~passed past passed~~ $\begin{cases} \text{past,} \\ \text{passed,} \end{cases}$
and the inevitable smoke and grime and dirt resting
heavily on the small cramped houses met Madge's eyes

Bridges they passed over, with the ~~inevitable~~ High
Street underneath, and they passed London Bridge.
(That's damn good, thought Anthony, you can sort of
feel the movement of the train and see the things passing.)

The train was slowing down. Victoria – of porters, and vans, and shouts, of buffets, and clocks, and glimpses of Grosvenor Street, of bookstalls, and men, and dirt, also of trains, ~~sometimes~~.

Strange confusion ~~of the in the~~ of the carriage. A man-to-man shake between Church and Army. An apology for Madge from the lady, stares from her ugly male progeny (Laughter and 'Damn good. Rather Dickensy', from Anthony), a clearance of the basket containing a kitten, which had been brought out during the journey, and to which everybody had said it was 'too sweet for words' and Madge springs ~~onto~~ on to the platform.'

Of course, thought Anthony, I shall have to revise all this, so I needn't go on crossing out. But the ideas are coming finely. They sort of come as you go along. Anthony continued:

~~There was a scuffle~~

~~When she got on to the platform~~

~~A porter came up~~ A porter found himself extremely concerned as regards the destination of ~~her~~ Madge's portmanteau.

Madge found herself mainly concerned about the presence of $\begin{cases} \text{Gordon} \\ \text{Phillip} \end{cases}$ at Victoria Station.

Here Anthony had to stop, because he didn't know much about Madge and Phillip or Gordon, or where they were going.

He lit a pipe over it, and puffed, and thought he would far rather be puffing a curved pipe over it, and in a moment decided to take a brooding stroll and buy a curved pipe, and come back and finish the chapter.

He took the stroll, trying hard to brood. This active exponent of the splendid adventure then found some more things to say to the interviewer, and some things he would write. 'The first chapter of "The Splendid Adventure",' he would write, 'is, perhaps, the worst chapter in any book I have yet read.' He would be well known for this witty self-depreciation.

He found the shops were shut, came in and went to his room, put the first of 'The Splendid Adventure' into a small top drawer, and ran downstairs saying 'Quite enough for my first night. I've made my initiation.'

The only addition to 'The Splendid Adventure' was made on the next evening. The curved pipe was no help after all. Anthony left it after short counsel with himself. He must go for a week swamping himself with the characters and the plot.

This was the addition:

Phillip and Madge met, shook hands, and made a decision about having tea. They went into the nearest tea-place.

Phillip ordered 'Tea, and bread and butter, and cakes.'

~~The waitress seemed surprised and astounded. There is surely nothing to equal the look of surprise a London waitress gives one when she is spoken to. One would imagine she had been asked for money rather then service. All she does is with an air of divine.~~

Chapter Seven

THE ACTOR

I

The right procedure, if you were a new arrival at the Fauconberg Hotel, was to sit quietly in the lounge, smile weakly at the jokes, not to speak, but to wait, and hope, till some intrepid and particularly chivalrous person spoke to you. If that happened you might make a diffident reply, and perhaps tell a very short story. Then you had to wait until somebody offered to play billiards or Bridge with you for the evening, or until Betty took you up. Soon you would be talked about as quite a nice new arrival, and interesting too, and soon you would be one of them.

You were certainly not to presume at the outset that a hotel was a hotel and that you had the same conversational rights as anybody else – the same conversational rights, for instance, as the the people who could remember Mr Braddon (they always called him Jackie; poor fellow; got killed in Soudan), or the people who remembered the hotel three years ago. (It was a far jollier place then. The life seemed to have gone out of it now, somehow.)

This is why Mr Brayne gave offence when he first arrived at the Fauconberg. Anthony found him, one morning a little before lunch, talking fluently and unconsciously to those around him, with no respect for conversational rights whatever.

Mr Sydney Brayne ('Not that I think myself very brainy on that account,' Mr Brayne would say) was a young, clean-shaven man of about twenty-one. He wore an oldish grey suit, oldish brown shoes, well polished, and oldish white spats. His hair was well plastered, but not cut much. His face, looked at from the front, or a little to right or left, was aquilinely quite all right. But sideways he had a nose. His teeth and hair were not too clean – but not really noticeably not too clean. He did not quite speak with a lisp. Not quite – but after a little of him you found yourself waiting for his 's's. His striped collar matched his striped shirt for seven days a week; but it was a soft collar and turned over some time about Thursday, showing a clean side.

He looked like an actor, and was one. For quite five months of the year he played leading juveniles in the provinces. He was a natural actor, and a quiet actor, quietly killing his play.

He had obtained his experience, in the first place, with

a Shakespearian Company. He had played black slaves, attendants, messengers, murderers, senators, citizens of Verona, physicians, and apparitions. This more or less supernumerary work was poor work, and Mr Brayne, dreamily banqueting upon his 'Petit Beurre' biscuit in Macbeth's sombre hall, would aspire to fuller parts. And he was given such parts after a year or so, having learnt to stamp, and fume, and sway, and moan, and rumble his rich voice in the preordained fashion. He had fallen badly in love with the dark girl who played Maria in 'Twelfth Night', with much waving of hands and quick chatter. ('She's a wonderful little actress too,' he said.)

Mr Brayne had two suits. A grey old suit, and a blue new one which had been new for a very long while. In the earlier part of the day the trousers of the grey suit had a distinct crease, but in the later part they had two vague creases. This was because he put his trousers under the mattress every night, rather carelessly, and the genuine crease will always assert itself. He did not wear the blue suit often, but then he wore a better collar and brushed his hair better. But you were not to think he was wearing his best suit ... He had an overcoat, too. It was too big for him; but it was a nice coat, greenish. You felt, as you looked at Brayne in it, that it had cost perhaps nearly eight pounds, and though it was too big Brayne had said, 'Well, the first and last duty of an overcoat is to keep you warm'. That is just what Brayne would have said. And he had an evening dress. When you first saw Brayne in his evening

dress you were not to be in the faintest way surprised that
he had an evening dress ...

You were not to be in the faintest way surprised at anything he *had* or *wore*. It would be possible to make positive
lists of things at which you were not to be in the faintest
way surprised:

1 pair white flannel trousers ⎫ (Worn with coat
1 pair white cricket boots ⎭ of new blue suit.)
1 plus-four costume. (Later.)
1 golden signet ring. (Twiddled during conversation.)
1 pipe. ('Got it in Bond Street, as a matter of fact.
    Expensive really, but worth the money.')
1 cigar. (Smoked in evening dress, in lounge, one
    night. Covert illness and spitting.)
Working knowledge of French language.
    (Demonstrated in 'Kommornt voo portay voo?'
    'May wee.' 'Shackern ar sorn goo.')
Certain knowledge of German language. (To Betty –
    'German for "I love you"? Eesh leeberleesh. Why?')

He was a gentleman. It transpired later (indeed it never
failed to transpire sooner or later) that the first Braynes
settled in Sussex somewhere about 1600. There was a
Sir *John* Brayne or something. Not a *Sir* John Brayne or
something. You were not to be in the faintest way surprised
that Brayne's direct forbears had been Knights in Sussex.
Besides, he had a gentleman's voice and bearing. But he

was no snob. He found stage carpenters, and costers, and people 'great fun'. He was educated at Hurstpierpoint College. He had been going to Winchester. He was very courteous to women.

Wherever he went Brayne had a name for being clever. He was supposed to be literary, too. And wherever he went Brayne saw to it that everybody should tumble to both these suppositions.

Shakespeare, was, to use his own phrase, 'religion with him'. He quoted him always, and alluded to him as 'Dear old Wully Shakespeer'. He sang. He had a good voice. It was the one thing at which you might be surprised. In high notes he half-closed his eyes and threw his chin up, and in low notes he frowned and dug his chin into his neck. He might be going to Italy to have his voice trained.

His people had intended him to go in for the Bar.

He went to the opera a good deal. 'Music is my one luxury,' he said. He only wished he could play some instrument.

'I have a very catholic taste in music,' he would often say. 'I can appreciate Beethoven and Darewski.' He said this often because he liked the word 'catholic' used this way. If you gave him half a chance he would have told you that the word 'catholic' need not necessarily be applied to the Roman Catholic Church. 'Catholic' simply meant 'Universal'. It might be the Roman *Universal* Church. Mr Brayne was full and free with information of that kind.

One thing more – there was a spring in the garden of

Brayne's aunt's house, and this spring was the source of the Thames. This was one of the first things that Brayne told you about himself, so no description of him would be quite complete without it.

When Anthony found Brayne in the lounge, he straightway engaged in conversational battle with him – a sort of literary race before the sounding of the gong for lunch.

Brayne had got well away with the grave-diggers' scene before Anthony had arrived. Anthony hovered a moment before challenging the stranger, then suddenly dashed in with 'Oh, yes, it's wonderful stuff, "Hamlet". But I like the first scene the best of the lot. The atmosphere in that first scene is simply wonderful. You know, "Who's there? Nay, answer me, stand and unfold yourself. Long live the King. Bernardo? He."'

'"You come most carefully upon your hour",' said Brayne, with a gesture.

'"'Tis now struck twelve",' said Anthony, '"get thee to bed, Francisco. For this relief much thanks, 'tis bitter cold, And I am sick at heart."'

'Oh, yes, it's simply wonderful stuff,' said Brayne, as though it were finished with now.

'"Have you had quiet guard?"' asked Anthony. '"Not a mouse stirring. Well, good night. If you do meet Horatio and Marcellus, The rivals of my watch bid them make haste." Oh, great.'

'Yes,' said Brayne, as though it were finished with now.

'"But look, the morn, in russet mantle clad"' said Anthony, '"Walks o'er the dew of yon high eastern hill."'

Now they were about level. A lady asked them what line in Shakespeare's 'Hamlet' the word *Kino* reminded them of. No one could think. 'A little more than kin and less than kind,' said the lady. 'Oh, that's very good,' said Brayne, 'I've never heard that before.' He, of all people, should have heard it.

Then Brayne dashed ahead with Bacon, and threw some light on what he called the Baconian heresy, and quoted people. Anthony held him with John Webster. Brayne ought to read 'The Duchess of Malfi'.

They came to more modern stuff. Brayne got away with Tchekoff and Brieux, but Anthony harried him with Dostoevski. '"Crime and Punishment",' he said. '"The Brothers Karamazov"—'

'No. I've never read them,' said Brayne.

'"The Idiot", "The House of the Dead", "Virgin Soil". No, that's Turgenev.'

'Have you read much Balzac?'

'"Eugénie Grandet"? "The Wild Ass' Skin"? Well, I don't know Balzac, as a matter of fact, so well as Stendhal.'

It took Brayne some time to pull round from Stendhal. He did it with heaps of O. Henry and a little Maupassant.

They were level again. Brayne made his final sprint with 'dear old Kit Marlowe', but Anthony flung out his breast and touched the tape first with Jeremy Taylor, just as the gong was heard.

'After all,' said Brayne, 'in the way of literature there's nothing to beat dear old Wully Shakespeer.'

Nevertheless, Anthony became a friend of Brayne. He lent Brayne five shillings, and Brayne would say that it was quite an intellectual tonic to talk to Anthony. It was so rare, he said, to meet somebody who had artistic feeling, who saw a little beyond the rut of ordinary things.

And one day Brayne offered to make Anthony an actor.

II

Brayne had a brother-in-law, whose name was Sewell. Brayne expected that Anthony had heard of him. He was the author of 'The Hungry Generations' – a play which had run in London for about five weeks. Sewell was now taking out a new play called 'The Coil' for a trial run in the provinces. Brayne was to play in this.

By the time he had started rehearsing Brayne was sitting at the same table as Anthony in the dining-room. And one night Brayne came back and said that the assistant stage manager of 'The Coil' had given up. Sewell was wanting another young man who could look well in evening dress, speak a few lines, and assist the stage manager, as soon as possible. Brayne had spoken to Sewell about Anthony, and Sewell had entertained the idea, and suggested that Anthony should be brought to him. 'Of course, perhaps you – er' said Brayne. 'Good heavens, no,' said Anthony, 'it's the very thing of all things I should like to do. I can never thank you enough for suggesting me, old man.'

So the next day Anthony was taken to a public house in Dean Street, Soho, in a room of which 'The Coil' was being rehearsed. He waited by the bar till Mr Sewell was brought down to him by Brayne.

Mr Sewell, like Mr Sladen, was the most agreeable person in the whole of the world, gave Anthony two drinks, and engaged him on the spot. Anthony was to assist the stage manager, play a small part, and have six pounds a week.

There were no end to the 'Thanks-awful-lies' to Mr Sewell, and no end of them to Brayne that night; and Anthony was head-hot with phrases for Diane, and there were Thinks and Dreams in bed that night.

It was the first night of a new play by Sewell, thought Anthony. Diane was in the stalls. Anthony was playing the principal part in the play. He was in his dressing-room, in his dressing-gown, making up. Sewell came in and shook his hand, and wished him luck. Sewell was white and nervous . . .

It was the moment before he went on. The play had been going very badly; the audience were restive. He made his entrance. He said his first line. The audience laughed happily and heartily. They did not laugh so much at the humour of the line as at the funny, natural way he said it. And for a quarter of an hour he had them exploding with laughter, not so much at the humour of the lines as at the funny, natural way he said them . . .

Then he changed. Towards the end of the act he had a tremendous pathetic scene with the girl, who was exquisitely pretty. (And Diane was in the stalls.) She was exquisitely pretty and very famous. Gladys Cooper, in fact. He had to kiss Gladys Cooper again and again. (And Diane was in the stalls.) The act ended in tumultuous applause ...

And all through the play he swayed them and pulled their hearts wherever he willed. And at the end the curtain went up again and again to tumultuous applause. The applause could not very well have been louder, but when Sewell told the audience that the credit of the play was not due to him but to Mr Forster the applause was doubled in power ...

Anthony stood in front of the curtain, and a deep hush came over the house. He made as if to speak, then with a humorous shy gesture dodged behind the curtain, to Homeric laughter and applause ...

He met Diane in the vestibule in front of the house. There was a thin crowd remaining. They were all having sly glances at him. They were delayed a few moments by Mrs Patrick Campbell and Basil Dean, who were unrestrained in their compliments, and to whom he introduced Diane. Mrs Patrick Campbell was a little cool to Diane, for which Anthony had to be correspondingly a little rigid with Mrs Patrick Campbell. Then he went into a taxi with Diane. 'Well – how do you think it went?' asked Anthony as the taxi moved away. 'Oh, Anthony, you were too wonderful for words. You know, Anthony, I don't think

I'm going to see you any more.' 'What do you mean?' 'I'll only be holding you back now.' Slowly he kissed her, and then said, 'Oh, Diane, do you love me at all now?' 'I do, Anthony.' The taxi jolted quickly on. Diane's cold hand was in his. The mauve lights of the thoroughfare sped across the inside of the taxi . . .

But apart from that, Anthony thought, as he found another cool place on his pillow, as regards Diane it was a capital thing to be going on the stage.

The 'Stage' implied to Anthony a flow of champagne, Bacchanalian orgies in the American Super-film manner, many delicious, silken young and youngish women, and a reprobate earl or so with a monocle . . . And to Diane such things could be hinted.

III

Anthony was the first to arrive at the rehearsal room the next morning. It was a large well-lit room with a bright red fire. At one end was a piano upon a small platform. Around the walls were many boards with names printed in gold upon them, and opposite the names a golden date. And on the walls were one or two large frames, thick-clustered with faded oblong photographs of high-collared men of Teutonic and blunt demeanour. There was a combined umbrella and hat-rack near the door.

Anthony was joined by two people who certainly didn't

look like actors, and they said 'Good morning' to Anthony without confidence, and all three talked weather and time for about five minutes.

Slowly the room filled with other people, who certainly didn't look like actors, and they all fell into little groups. Anthony was left alone. Mr Sewell arrived, talking hard with a tall, grey-headed man with a rimless monocle and a bow-tie which went twice round his collar. They went to a window by themselves.

A man came up to Anthony and said, 'Mr Forster, I believe?'

'That's right.'

'You're going to assist me, I understand, Mr Forster,' said the man, leering rather.

'Yes – rather,' said Anthony.

'Well, I hope we'll get on very well together, Mr Forster,' said the man, and shook Anthony's hand on it. 'It's not a very difficult show.'

'Oh, isn't it? Good,' said Anthony.

'I'll find up your part for you.'

'Oh, thanks awfully.'

The man went to a bag and brought Anthony a thin type-written script, bound with red paper.

'Thanks awfully,' said Anthony.

Trouble first came in the middle of the morning. The stage manager came over and whispered to him.

'Would you take out listerops azay strike you?' whispered the stage manager. 'I might miss something which you see.'

'Sorry. I'm deaf. Would you say the first part again?'

'List*props*'

'Damn sorry. I can't hear.'

'List of *props*.'

'Oh, *I* see,' said Anthony, but he didn't see at all, because he didn't know what a prop was.

'You see, I might miss something, and we want to get all the things ready by Saturday.'

'Yes – rather,' said Anthony.

The stage manager moved away. Anthony looked in front of him, speculating wildly. Soon he noticed that the stage manager was putting half an eye on him every minute or so. At last he saw the stage manager tearing a piece of paper from his large note-book. He came over, gave this to Anthony, and said, 'Have you got a pencil?'

'Yes, thanks,' said Anthony. 'Thanks.'

He brought out his pencil, put the bit of paper on his knee in full preparedness, and waited, until that time, perhaps, when a prop would strike him, as the stage manager had said it would.

The stage manager was still giving him a sidelong, suspicious glance ... So Anthony wrote at the top of his bit of paper 'PROPS' in neat capital letters which took a long while to make. And later 1, 2, 3, 4, 5, 6, 7, 8, 9, 10, and so on all down the page. All was ready for the props.

Then the stage manager came over to him, and looked at his bit of paper. 'How are you getting on?' he whispered.

'Well, as a matter of fact, I'm getting a bit muddled. I say, what *is* a prop exactly?'

'Oh, all right,' said the stage manager, 'don't worry about it.' And he walked away again.

At one o'clock they finished the rehearsal. There was some hanging about and listless chatting. The stage manager said, loudly, 'We'll start on Scene 2, Act 1, two-thirty this afternoon, please.' One of the actors stayed to speak to the stage manager; Mr Sewell continued his earnest conversation with the man in the bow-tie. Most of the rest went downstairs to the bar, where they sat on high chairs, drinking. Anthony went out to have his lunch, without his previous enthusiasm.

IV

Three days later Mr Sewell gave Anthony two more drinks, and took the assistant stage management away from him. There was nothing wrong, said Mr Sewell, Anthony had done very well, but he had not had quite enough experience. The salary would be reduced to four pounds. Anthony was delighted.

V

As a week passed Anthony became quite intimate with some of the members of 'The Coil' company. He learnt some of the ways of actors from them. He learnt that an actor's cigarettes and matches are his neighbour's, and that you weren't really supposed to say even plain 'Thank you' for them. He learnt that the first thing to be done with an actor is to go and have a drink, and the next thing to have another. And he learnt that you didn't say, 'Thanks awfully,' when the actor paid for it, and suggest that you should pay your share, but paused awhile until he said 'Well – cheerio,' and then drank. And when the drink was finished you didn't say, 'Let me pay for some more drinks now, in return,' but you said, 'What are you taking?' and the actor probably said, 'Bitter,' and you said, 'Two bitters, please,' to the barmaid. And when a third actor came in and said, 'Well, what are you two going to have?' you didn't say, 'I don't think I'll have any more. I've had two bitters already and my head's feeling rather funny, and anyway it'll be frightfully expensive for you to pay for drinks for both of us,' but you said, 'I'll have another bitter, I think.'

Chapter Eight

THE TRAIN JOURNEY

I

The play opened at Sheffield. The train call for the journey was on a Sunday at eight o'clock.

This first journey on tour is a very telling journey. The spites and enmities, more or less shadowily present at the rehearsals, now take a definite and fully-recognised character.

There is an air of jealous criticism and unuttered self-assertion from the very beginning. There are distinctions to be made ... To begin with there is the great Salary distinction. So unaffected is this that the truly great salaries mostly come down by a later train. And there are a thousand other unacknowledged little hostilities. Hostilities, for instance, between those who bear golf-clubs on their shoulders, and those who do not; between those who have lunch on the train, and those who do not; between those who set out with undreamed-of personal sandwiches and apples, and those who cannot do so. There is even a kind of hostility between those who travel by one compartment and those who travel by another. Each compartment has been rearing its own warm, smoke-ridden atmosphere. One has been discussing Spiritualism, another the Melvilles and Mrs Kimberley, another has been devoting itself wholly to solo whist. Exclusiveness comes of this. Compartment pride ... Perhaps most unpopular of all is the carpenter, who goes into a distinct compartment with an amazingly pretty wife, for a carpenter, and a baby. The prettiness of the carpenter's wife brings about much resentment.

It is not necessary to say that Mr Brayne intended to spend his journey with the best salaries he could. But he was handicapped by his particularly heavy bag and went a little too late into the best salaries to ask them, in easy tones, if there was any room for him. The best salaries said, 'Well – it'll be rather a crush, old boy', and Mr Brayne, wishing to thrust himself upon no society, and reflecting that he could certainly obtain a better conversational stronghold with the next best salaries, stumbled out again. The next best salaries, however, had erected a table for whist and had no room for Mr Brayne at all. Thus Mr Brayne was unhappily constrained to spend his journey with the lower salaries, or understudies. In such an environment, he resolved, he would endeavour to hold no conversational standing at all, but read his newspaper.

In this compartment there were seven persons altogether. There was Mr Brayne, and there was Anthony, who had aspired to nothing better.

There was Miss Robins, who played Mrs Shenstone. It was a very small part, and she understudied as well. Miss Robins had a homely face.

There was Miss Anderson, who played the maid and understudied. Her gift had hitherto been spent solely upon team work in the musical drama, and this was her first appearance in 'legitimate'. Her face was not very pretty, but then it was not very homely.

There was Mr Gallagher (Miss Anderson often merrily called him Mr Shean), who played the Butler. This was by no means his first appearance in the legitimate drama. It was indeed thirty-seven years since that event. He was an Irishman, a Roman Catholic, the owner of a head full of years and tolerant wisdom, and overlain by abundant snowy hair, these characteristics conspiring to make his attitude at once consciously and conscientiously fatherly. His speech was accordingly ponderous. He was for ever addressing the second party with a measured 'Lady', 'Son', 'My Son', 'My Friend', followed by a fatherly *bon mot*. You were expected to remember what he said even into distant years. 'As dear old Gallagher used to say to me,' you would then be expected to say, '"My Son—"' Sometimes he was brighter though, and told funny Irish tales. He had once been a raconteur professionally, you understood. You were listening to the real thing. He told his stories very rapidly, with all the words and sentences running against each other (Sure-sez-Paddy-an'-Paddy-goes-off-an'-meets-Mike-Mike-sez-Paddy-What-sez-Mike), so that you couldn't quite hear what *had* been said, laughed outright three times before that was proper, and indeed kept up some uncertain sniggering throughout. Miss Anderson thought Mr Gallagher was a dear old man. The other two people in the compartment were an oldish lady who did not belong to the company of actors, and the young man who played Colonel Goring's black servant. The former had a nice corner and was very quiet, occasionally enjoying a demonstration of not being able to help smiling at the funny things that were said. The latter was not going to get his effect of the black servant by mere grease-paint, his parents having given him the fuzzy hair and colour in the first place. He was called all sorts of things by the members of the company – 'The Indian', 'The Hindu', 'The Negro', 'The Nigger', 'The Dark Gentleman', 'The Swarthy Gentleman', 'Our Asiatic Friend'. Miss Anderson abruptly called him the 'Blackie'. But 'Good heavens, lady, you mustn't call him that,' said Mr Gallagher. 'The fellow's a gentleman.' And the rest of the company were one with Mr Gallagher. It was widely understood that These People can be devilishly proud.

Mr Karshi was indeed proud, but perhaps as much of his own recent attainments as of race. He was a law student, as well as an actor, having successfully passed many examinations. He put his accomplishments to their fullest use, not alone by freely handing on to his acquaintances countless tit-bits of his acquired erudition, but by a usefully meticulous punctilio for the letter of the law. He had already sued his last manager in a question of contract, and was in the course of suing his present manager in a question of salary. At the moment, to judge by a certain rigid arrangement of his lips, it seemed something more than possible that the railway company, if they weren't careful, would also be in for some nasty litigation ... Mr Karshi had suing blood in him.

As the train slid quietly and unceremoniously from the station the mental atmosphere was most clear and friendly. Proper conversation had not commenced. There had been nothing but the most amiable adjustment of feet and accommodation of bags. Mr Gallagher had given his corner to Miss Robins with his usual slow courtesy. Miss Anderson said Anthony was a poor dear, and she was sure she was squashing him. There was perhaps one little cloud, a very little one. Miss Robins had a large red book unashamed upon her knee. It was called 'Psycopathology of Everyday Life'. Psycopathology? Now that would plainly have to be dealt with sooner or later ...

There was no bright talk to begin with, though the newspapers had not yet been opened, except by the lady in the corner. They were all, perhaps, a little amazed by the length of the journey in front of them, and the sordid environment of the railway. There were endless horrid black villas and yellow hoardings under the grey, humid day. There were children in the yards behind the villas, and women at work. Hard, patchy work, with no expectation whatever of eventual triumph over the dirt and disorder. The women did not watch the train go by. And they seemed a little grotesque and remote to the people in the train, for they were so noiseless from in here with the measured beat of the engine and the oiled clatter of wheels. Dream people . . .

The actors were now facing each other for ordered scrutiny, and tacit advantage was taken of it on all sides . . . Noses were found, complexions, rings, good clothes and shabby, vulgar clothes . . .

Miss Robins' eyes rested angrily once or twice on Miss Anderson's fur coat. Miss Anderson looked tired, lay back, smiled feebly at her gesture to Anthony . . .

Then suddenly they were all bright. Miss Robins had some snapshots and began to hand them round. They were good snapshots, of Miss Robins; Miss Robins and a young man; or Miss Robins, a young man and a motorcycle. One showed Miss Robins seated alone on a motorcycle. Miss Robins was always smiling, and so was the young man. Miss Robins looked a shade more handsome than she looked in the train that day. Save perhaps in one snapshot, where she had a very queer appearance, and there was a photographic blob about her mouth. The young man held a pipe firmly in his mouth, and was plainly an open-air young man. The snapshots were taken in perfectly lovely places, on windy downs, under fresh trees, by ruined walls.

'This is me,' said Miss Robins, 'engaged in my favourite pursuit of dashing about the country on the back of a motor bike.' The assembled company were not troubled by the remotest inward questioning as to whether the homeliness of Miss Robins' face might have shut her off from such pleasures ...

After the snapshots Miss Robins found, to her surprise, that she had also some photographs proper in her bag, and she was persuaded to show them too. These were exclusively of young men – nearly handsome and ever immaculate. Nevertheless, one young man was undeniably ugly. 'He's an awfully nice boy,' said Miss Robins.

'He's just gone up to Cambridge,' she added.

But Miss Anderson, who had suffered the snapshots, was not going to have that.

'I know a boy at Cambridge,' said Miss Anderson; 'I had a letter from him two days ago.'

'Oh, yes?' said Anthony.

'Yes, he's an awfully nice boy. But he will keep on writing me asking me to give up the stage. I keep on telling him nothing in the world'd make me give up my Work. But he won't listen. He keeps on writing. I mean, it's so absurd, isn't it?'

'Oh, yes,' said Anthony. 'Rotten ...'

After this there was silence.

Mr Gallagher handed back the last of the photographs to Miss Robins with a pleasant smile and 'Thank you, dear lady. Very nice indeed', and there was another silence.

Reading was gently implied. They rattled their newspapers open. Miss Robins opened the 'Psycopathology of Everyday Life' about the middle and Mr Karshi made an immediate mute challenge by fumbling in his bag and bringing to light a heavy volume of Stubbs. Miss Anderson, however, made the challenge direct. She leant over to Miss Robins.

'What on earth are you reading, my dear?' said Miss Anderson. 'The Fizziothology of Everyday Life? My word, how on earth can you?'

'Why, I find it exceedingly interesting,' said Miss Robins.

'Oh, no doubt you do. But it's beyond me altogether. I should go mad if I tried to read all that highbrow stuff. It's all right for those who like it. But it's beyond me, I must say. Do you like that sort of thing, Mr Forster?'

'Oh. I don't know . . . ' said Anthony, on neither side.

Mr Karshi, who had only Mr Gallagher between him and Miss Robins, now thrust his elegant dark hand over on to Miss Robins' book. 'Ah? Yess?' he said. 'Very in-ter-resting', smiled and nodded.

Mr Brayne had also to assert himself. 'What's that you've got? A book about Psychology. You must let me read that after you.'

Mr Gallagher rolled a cigarette.

'I've got lots of books at home,' said Miss Anderson, in her inconsequent way. 'I'm simply a voracious reader. I read morning, noon and night. I'm not so bad as I used to be, but I used to be simply awful. Such a weird conglomeration too. Nothing like that, though. That's beyond me.' Miss Anderson plainly wished to enforce her stringently lowbrow attitude.

'I suppose,' said Mr Brayne, 'that the works of Mr William le Queux or Phillips Oppenheim are rather more after your fancy?'

But that was impolite, and made some palpable confusion in the compartment. There was no answer. Anthony blushed.

'Not that I don't think detective fiction isn't great fun,' Mr Brayne tactfully amended. 'The adventures of the redoubtable Mr Sherlock Holmes and his trusty friend Watson simply enthral me.' But there was only another silence.

'I've just been lent the most wonderful book,' said Miss Robins. '"The Undying Fire", by H. G. Wells.'

'Oh, yes, I've read that,' said Anthony. 'Jolly good, isn't it?'

'Yes, isn't it? It's a very short book for Wells, isn't it?'

'Yes – it *is* short.'

'Wells?' asked Miss Anderson. 'He writes awful scientific books, doesn't he?'

'He certainly has Great Imaginative Power,' Mr Brayne allowed. 'His books like "The War of the Worlds" are first-rate literature, in their way. But as far as I can see the fellow's developed into a Rampant Socialist nowadays.'

'He's a frightful Atheist too, isn't he?' asked Miss Anderson. 'Him and Bernard Shaw.'

Mr Gallagher had been unsuccessful in rolling his cigarette, and was having another go. Mr Karshi was smiling and sensitively attentive.

'His chapter on Spiritualism in "The Undying Fire," said Miss Robins to Anthony, 'is awfully amusing, isn't it? I don't know that I quite fall in with him, but it's very well done.'

'Yes. It's brilliant, isn't it?'

'Do you believe in Spiritualism?' asked Miss Anderson, 'I don't. A boy asked me to a seance the other night, but I wouldn't go. It's such a shame, because he's such an awfully nice boy otherwise. But he's mad on this spiritualism. I think I'll go one night, just for fun.'

'No, young lady, keep away from it,' said Mr Gallagher. 'Keep away from it.'

'Oh, I don't see the harm of it, if it's done in a Scientific and Inquiring Spirit,' said Mr Brayne.

'No,' said Mr Gallagher. 'No. It's away from God. It's away from God.'

That led Miss Anderson's butterfly brain to other considerations.

'I'm awfully wicked,' she said. 'I haven't been to church for centuries. Isn't it frightful of me?'

'I don't think it's a bit frightful of you,' said Anthony. 'I don't go to church and I don't intend to.'

'Oh, don't you believe in God, Mr Forster?' asked Miss Anderson, all excited.

'Well, not the conventional Christian God.'

'You're an Agnostic then,' said Mr Brayne.' Well, there's a case to be made for the Agnostic.'

'Don't you believe in the *Bible*, Mr Forster?' Miss Anderson persisted. 'Not in Adam and Eve, and Gnaw's Ark, and all those?'

'No – certainly not.'

'But you must believe in *God*, Mr Forster? You must believe in *God*. *You* know. There must be *something*. I mean, how did things *come*? They must have *come some-how*. There must be a *God*.'

'Oh, I don't deny there's a God. But I don't believe in a magical sort of God that created the world in seven days. I think things evolved.'

Mr Gallagher came in here firmly with his *bon mot*.

'Young man, we think like you very often when we're at your age, but the older we get, a closer sense of that Great Mind of Creation is brought home to us.'

'Well, I'm sure I'll never believe in that sort of God, however old I get.'

'You go on thinking it, my boy,' Mr Gallagher replied generously. 'You go on thinking it. But you'll remember my words, son, one of these days.'

'But I'm not saying I don't believe in God. All I say is that I don't believe in miracles. I say, whatever is, is natural, that's all.'

'Do you believe?' began Miss Anderson, and, 'You speak of miracles' began Mr Gallagher. 'Go on, young lady,' said Mr Gallagher. 'No, it's nothing important,' said Miss Anderson. 'No, do go on.'

'I was only going to say,' Miss Anderson ventured parenthetically, 'do you believe we're all descended from monkeys?'

'Yes,' said Anthony. 'I do.' And there was a little silence.

'I was going to say,' resumed Mr Gallagher, 'you talk of miracles? What isn't a miracle? Isn't it miracle enough that you and I should be here? Isn't all God's nature a miracle? Aren't all the birds of the air and the beasts of the field miracles, my boy?'

'Yes, I know it's all wonderful, and all that. All I say is that I don't believe there's a personal God that interferes magically with the universe.'

'You young men come along with your Evolution and your Wells and your Science, and you say you don't believe in God, and that you don't—'

'I didn't say that, but still—'

'Don't believe in this, and don't believe in that. But it's all wrong. It's all wrong. You say there's a God, but no personal God. But, young man, do you mean to tell me you can't see the great Personal Mind behind it all? Why, boy, what are you thinking about? Isn't the whole working of the Great Machine living proof of the Glory of God? Think, my boy, think.' Mr Gallagher now became wholly rhetorical. 'Look around you at the wonders and works and beauties of Nature', he continued, indicating with a sweep of his hand fields and fields of dumped motor-lorries. 'Is that not sufficient proof for you? Someone has thought of all that, my young friend. Some great First Cause has made the glory of the morning and the stars of night under heaven's peace. Someone has made the Spring, and the flowers, the wealth of Summer, and the leaves rustin' in Autumn. Someone,' he perorated with a gallant flourish to Miss Anderson, 'has thought of your own pretty face, my dear.'

The thought tickled Miss Anderson.

'Yes,' said Anthony, struggling. 'I'm not denying the beauty of it all, for a moment. All I say is that there's no miraculous element in it. For instance, in Christianity I don't believe in some of the legends about Jesus.'

There was no reply to this.

'You see,' he continued. 'If you go into it all historically (Renan and Strauss and all that), you can see the historical origins of all these legends. The idea of the Trinity and all that.'

Anthony was quite bright again now. But he was not to have his say. It was Mr Karshi's turn. Mr Karshi had been lifting his hand, and limply opening his mouth in preparation for the last five minutes, but they had been too quick for him. This time he pounced.

'Now—' he began, raised that slender dark hand with authority, and waited a moment to let them register his introduction into the discussion. 'Now. I am Church of Ing-land.'

'Oh, are you?' cried a startled Miss Anderson, but recovered herself immediately. Just the sort of things a Blackie would be really ... He must have been converted or something. Miss Anderson's undisciplined mind was visited by an astounding flash picture of the conversion of Mr Karshi. A nude, glossy, missionary-consuming Mr Karshi, harangued from his gruesome brewing-pot and desert palm-tree ...

'Yes,' Mr Karshi endorsed. 'I am Church of Ing-land.' His tone was impartial, but final.

'Now what I say is why – er—' He was a little bothered by all the silence and expectancy. 'Er – what I say is why, why thee Churches cannot be one. Now if we inquire into History we find thee causes of it. Now what are thee causes of all this diverse-ness? Lewther. Martin Lewther. Now Lewther was first a member of thee Roman Catholic Church. But he want too marry, and thee Catholic Church are given to celi-basee – which mean – unmarriedness. Now what does Lewther do? He attend the Diet of Worms.'

Miss Anderson again checked a swift urgency for comment. But they *did* do quaint things in History!

'Now what is thee result?' continued Mr Karshi. 'Lewther he break away from the Established Church. They call it thee Reformation. Now Henry the Eight of Ing-land, what does he do? He up till now – he call himself Feedayee Defensor – which is thee Defendor of Faith. Now what is the character of Henry the Eight? He is avaricious man. He want money. Now what does he do? He see Lewther break away from thee Pope, and he follow, for then he can sack thee monas-tries. Also he want a new wife.'

'Oh, did he?' said Miss Anderson, in a hoity-toity way,

'Yes. He tired with Catherine of Aragon. Now he see his chance. He – er – er – sack thee monas-tries, and – er – he is divorce. He marry Anne Bolinn – who is lady of Court. Afterward he execute her. She is his two – second wife. Now – er – what does Henry do? Ing-land is declare Protestant.

'But there is not only thee Reformation. By no mean.' Mr Karshi's listeners had guessed as much. 'No, by no mean – means. There is thee Renay-sornce. Thee Greek scholars. They are spreading learning. There is Thomas More who write an "Utopia" There is Colet who found thee Paul's School. There is Erasmus who – er – write – many books. He write a Latin Syntax. He a Dutchman – from Holland. But he spend time at English University – of Oxford.'

'Yes. Yes,' said Mr Gallagher, and nodded, shifting his legs.

'Now what does Erasmus do? He – er – is a scholar. He help bring about the Vaken-ing of learning in Europe.'

Here Anthony's stick dropped on to the floor, previously touching Miss Anderson's toes. 'I'm awfully sorry,' said Anthony. 'I thought that was going to happen,' said Miss Anderson, but Mr Karshi held his own.

'Also there is Calvin,' he said. 'He is oppose to Arminius. Arminius – he another Dutchman. Calvin. He believe in predestination. He believe we are either predestined to Heaven or Hell. Now Arminius. He – er. Not think that. There are thee Calvinists and thee Arminians. Now Knox? He a Scotch, Now if you read Carlyle he include him as one of his hair-roes in his book "Thee Hair-roes and thee Hair-roe Worshippers." Knox. He come later . . . '

'Well, I think,' said Anthony, 'it'd be better if we set up a different Church altogether.'

'And what Church would you set up in its stead, my Young Atheist Friend?' asked Mr Gallagher, still slowly benign, but surely losing patience. 'The Anthony Forster Church?'

They all laughed.

Anthony flushed.

'No, young man. The Church of Christ will survive yours, I think you'll find.'

'But I didn't *say* I wanted to set up an Anthony Forster Church. I simply— All I say is that all the superstitions and things of the Church are so *damn silly.*'

'Well, whatever we think, I think we shouldn't forget the presence of the ladies, young man.' A sterner note.

'Damn isn't swearing. But really. Don't you see what I mean? Don't *you* agree with me, Miss Robins?'

But Miss Robins was given no time to answer.

'"The fool hath said in his heart",' began Mr Gallagher, and, 'I mean you've only got to study—' began Anthony. '"In his heart that there is no God",' continued Mr Gallagher. 'And I think we all ought to remember that.'

'Well, I think it's only fools who believe in superstitions,' said Anthony.

'There's no need at all to get personal,' said Mr Gallagher, raising his voice, and, 'You've only got to study Comparative Religion,' said Anthony, at exactly the same time. He, of course, had to raise his voice too.

Mr Karshi came to their aid with further scholarly historical commentary, happily combining tact and pleasure.

II

The train came in at a station. There were twenty minutes to wait. Anthony got out and went to the bar. He was very hungry and thirsty. He wanted a cup of tea, though manly pride urged him to have beer. He bought a cup of tea and sat by a comforting fire. The room began to fill with the company of the revue 'Yes, Let's,' which was travelling by the same train. Predominant was a man in a heavy black coat with an astrakhan collar and a bowler hat. A forlorn man, wholly preoccupied by last Saturday's uncompromising returns ... There were men who wore shapely, shabby grey coats with velvet collars and white silk mufflers; and there was a darkness on their eyebrows and a vague ochrish colour on their faces suggesting ineradicated Saturday night grease-paint. There was one young man with a sporty cap and a yellow waistcoat. But the girls were in the majority. They were faint, frail, pretty girls, with white faces more bad-tempered than sad. Their dresses were not shabby in certain dull lights, though the blue ones (rubbed vigorously with a rag arid hot water from a saucer) had collected a lot of dust. For the moment it seemed that Life and their chosen profession had the upper hand of the company of 'Yes, Let's'.

One of the girls came and sat down near Anthony. She seemed to be turning her back on the others. Once another girl came up to her and said, 'How are you, May?' and May said, 'I'm all right, thanks'. Then an elderly woman came up to her and said, 'Where've you been getting to, May?' And May said, 'Oh – nowhere.' 'What's the matter with you, deer?' asked the elderly woman. 'It's that Mrs Jacoby.' 'What's she been doing?' 'Saying "fancy going with that old man", like that.' 'My dear, you musern't listen to what people say.' 'I can't help it.' 'You musern't take things so seeriously, deer; it don't do.' And the elderly woman sidled away.

About five o'clock they slid into Sheffield. Anthony met the advance manager, who gave him the address of a combined room he had found for him in the town. Anthony, weighed down with golf-clubs and heavy bag, asked his way from street to street. It was twilight. Twilight may turn London to purple beauty, but never Sheffield.

The splendid adventurer was more than usually depressed, and still sullenly ruminating upon the squabble with Mr Gallagher. He had a quaint sense that something had been left undone . . .

He walked stupidly through littered, greasy street after littered, greasy street. 'Where the hell *is* this road?' he said.

Why hadn't the Robins woman supported him?

Old Gallagher had started being rude.

Was 'damn' swearing?

Chapter Nine

SHEFFIELD

I

His combined room was at a black house in a smoky street. He was taken into a black passage by an untidy, cheerful landlady, with eyes like little black beetles, and they climbed the black stairs to his combined room. Here it was observed that the weather was much colder, that the train was late, that it had been raining all that morning in Sheffield, that the English climate was fickle, that Anthony should be brought tea and bread and butter.

This was brought to him after five minutes, and after five more minutes some milk, by a sluttish girl of about nineteen. Innumerable 'Thanksawfullies'.

He drank the tea and tried to read 'The Fruitful Vine', by Robert Hichens, which he had found on his dressing-table.

Then he walked about his room, looking at it. The wallpaper shouted roses around green trellis. There was a huge bed; a photograph, framed in wood, of a family, wickedly ugly; and to each side of this photograph two big prints, enframed too – one of a lady, in shadow, receiving news of her husband's death at the front, while her child, in sunlight, plays with tin soldiers on the floor; and the other of the same, soldier returning, in defiance of Government telegrams, to the same lady through a small garden gate, and there are many roses about. There was a washing stand with a jug and basin still shouting roses.

There was a large mantelpiece, with rosy ornaments, and a fireplace set far back, for the chimney's comfort. The green pallor of the incandescent mantle augmented the tawdry cheerlessness of the whole.

Anthony thought that he would like to go out to see the town. But he would have to tell his landlady if he did that; and he didn't know her name, or in which door of those black passages downstairs she dwelt. And if he went downstairs he might meet the girl, and he couldn't very well say, 'Will you tell your mother I'm going out, but I'll be back in time for supper?' Perhaps she wasn't the landlady's daughter, and perhaps the landlady didn't mean to give him supper.

On the whole it was best to wait, and if the landlady didn't come up to him, he would wait till ten, and then go to bed. And if she came up when he was in bed he would say, 'Oh, I've gone to bed. I'm very tired after the journey . . . ' And that was that. He continued 'The Fruitful Vine' . . .

There was a knock at his door, and the girl came in and started to clear away the tea-things. Speechlessness, and eloquent clattering.

'Are there any cinemas open on Sunday here?' asked Anthony.

'Ah bleeve there's woon oop by station, with Charlie in "Pilgrim". Ah bleeve 'tis very good.'

'Yes, I believe it is.'

More speechlessness and eloquent clattering, broken suddenly by the girl.

'Ma says will ye be in before half-past ten or she'll give ye key?'

'Oh, I'll be in all right. Thanks awfully.'

The girl left. Very happily Anthony put on his hat and coat. He was not only allowed to go out until half-past ten; it was the presumption.

He arrived at the cinema in the middle of 'The Pilgrim'. After that came episode No. 14 of 'The Arrow of the Gods', entitled 'The Lake of Fire', and dealt with disturbances between a Ruth and Tom and a hooded, mysterious airman. When the two principal people of the story were fallen half-way down a precipice, they asked, 'How Did Ruth And Tom Escape From The Black Abyss?' 'Ooooooo!' exclaimed the onlookers, and knowing comments came that 'It always switches off just when you're most excited. That's to bring you here next week.' Nevertheless the audience were more or less complacent, being inwardly satisfied that there was really no Abyss so Black but that Ruth and Tom would Escape from It.

Then came Pathé, Lloyd George, and King George and the Prince of Wales, attentively amiable and smiling delightfully.

Then a comedy, with eggs and flour dispersed, and much skyscraper climbing.

And then the English Super-film 'The Wages of Love'. This did not interest Anthony much, and after about half an hour it seemed surely foredoomed that the young heroine would soon be knitting tiny socks, and be kissed by her mother, or saying, 'Don't you see? I can't – *now*' which is cinematographic for 'I am going to have a child.' And Anthony didn't care, so he came out.

He came out and came straight upon some middle-salaried male members of the company of 'The Coil' who were gaily but conscientiously intent upon their Sunday evening pub crawl. That Anthony should leave them was out of the question. They held his arms. So trying hard to remember the direction of the combined room, he was taken to the theatre, outside which a happy conference was held, and then to a little public house near to it. And he was given four half-pints of beer and a double whisky. Just as he had finished some quick arithmetic, and was going to ask everybody what they would have ... 'Time' was shouted amid the bawling, and the actors sidled mechanically out into the street, and had another happy conference in the middle of it.

It was resolved, between the story-telling, that they should all go to a public house a little way off, where drinks were served after time. Anthony said, 'I think I'll be getting along. I've lost my way already.' An actor said, 'Rot, man, it's only ten, and yon can ask your way back, can't you?' 'I suppose I can,' said Anthony.

The public house was shut and showed no sign of the belated revelry desired. Entrance was made, however, by a side door, after much knocking and rattling of bolts. Anthony and the actors were taken, conspirators, into a smallish room.

The room was laden with heat from the fierce golden fire, and grey with cigarette smoke. A few big tables, and behind them men and women, sitting up against the walls, all round. On the tables coarse tumblers filled, half-filled, quarter-filled, or dregged with clear brown beer, frothing limply at the top. And beer had been spilt on to the tables. Little pools of it, and half-circles, and old stains of pools and half-circles. The landlord sat in front of the fire, sweating generously.

There was a confused, loud mumble of talk, which would die slowly while a man told them a funny tale, or while two men held a senseless banter from each end of the room, or while the landlord rose and gave them a rhyme or limerick, which did not hurt Anthony so much for its own abandoned villainy, but because of the women there.

At such times they would all listen, watching the speaker with a malicious droop of the eyes. And at every muddy sally the women would laugh just a little louder than the men, to show *they* liked it just as much ...

In all their speech there was the spirit of an almost defined enmity to God, with whom they connected Jesus. Jesus had a place in every other phrase of theirs, and was represented in many unclean images. Their attitude was less one of cheery unbelief than that of a God admitted and to be blamed, with happy venom. In another age Anthony might have awaited a sudden Confusion on these people – an Avenging Angel or a Flaming Cross.

As it was, Anthony was beginning to find that he was getting seriously affected by the beer, and began framing phrases for Diane – about taking to drink, and wounded love being the cause of it, and all Diane's responsibilities. And two more double whiskies were passed to him, and he never thought of not taking them.

Soon a table and an actor started swimming firmly for his forehead, and he started little exercises in looking really perfectly straight at the landlord. He said at last to an actor, 'I think I'm going.' The actor said, 'Rot, you'll have another drink, and then I'll come with you. This is just where one begins to feel a bit merry.' But after the next drink the actor showed no inclination to go. Anthony said, 'Are you coming?' 'Soon, old boy.' Anthony stumbled to a man who was standing in the doorway.

'Do you know how I can get to Cloff, or Cluff, or Clow

or something road?' he said. 'It's spelt See, ell, oh, yoo, jee, aich.'

The man said, 'Yes', and unbolted doors. When outside he said, 'Ye go down here, ye see, and ye go along t'right, till ye come to Winchester Rowed, ye see? Ye go down Winchester Rowed, till ye come to tramlines, an' church an' all. Then ask agen. Ye're not far then.'

'I've got you,' said Anthony. 'Thanks.'

'Or ye might go simpler way. Ye might go down here t'left, and straight on down till ye come to tramlines, an' follow tramlines till ye find Clough Rowed. Ye might go that way.'

'Yes, I think I will,' said Anthony. 'Thanks.'

'Ye might find that way simpler.'

'Yes, I might. Thanks.'

Ten minutes' unsteady roving brought Anthony no nearer to tramlines. His legs were not affording their usual loyal support; but he was happy and contented.

He asked another man. 'Now, let me see, where are we?' said the man.

'Sheffield,' said Anthony.

'You'd better go down here till you get to the tramlines. And then follow them up to Clough Road. You can't miss it.'

'Thanks very much.'

'We must keep the balance,' he said to himself. 'We must keep the balance. The balance must be kept, at all costs.'

He found the tramlines, followed them, but found no

Clough Road. He asked another man – a small man walking very quickly on his way. 'Yes, it's third on left,' said the small man. 'If ye're walkin' that way I'll come with you.'

They walked together silently and quickly. 'I've just come up from London,' said Anthony.

The little man said, 'Oh, have you?' and did not seem very interested, but started to talk very quickly and merrily. Anthony only listened to bits. 'Just come away ... the band, ye know ... one or two drinks ... always full of hospitality ... quite merry and happy in spite of things.'

'Do I look drunk?' asked Anthony, 'because you are.'

Then, all in a muddle, Anthony saw the face of the small man looking at him very earnestly, and speaking no more.

'After all, it's best to be frank,' said Anthony, quietly.

The earnest face was seen telling him that it would be all right, and that they were nearly at Clough Road now, and vanished.

Anthony fancied he could discern the corner of Clough Road swaying grandiosely in the distance. He made for it, lifting his legs high, and prancing – a delightfully effortless operation in his present condition.

'I'm a War Horse,' he said.

At the corner of Clough Road he leant against a lamp-post, for five minutes, looking at his shoes. 'This must stop,' he said. 'This must stop.'

He would go on being a War Horse till he reached the first lamp-post in Clough Road, but then it must stop.

He was a War Horse, within the exact limit appointed.

It was too dark to see the numbers of the houses. He chose a house. No knocker. He banged with his fist on the door. A young man opened the door after some time.

'Is this where I live?' asked Anthony.

'I don't think so,' hazarded the young man, and then shut the door rather quickly. Anthony chose another house.

'Ah, here ye are at last,' said his landlady.

'Yes,' said Anthony. 'The Return of the Wanderer.'

On the black stairs he tripped noisily, 'How do you spell this road?' he asked; 'that is to say "pronounce"?'

His landlady brought him some bread and cheese, and cocoa.

'I hope I'm not late,' said Anthony.

'Ah, well, what does it matter so long as it was a nice girl!' She laughed at this, and Anthony joined in, with the air of one who says, 'We two understand each other perfectly, don't we?'

II

The morning broke on Sheffield windy and pure, a blue sky and massive clouds, dazzling by whiteness.

Anthony, pale-faced, his eyes aching and a clinging taste in his mouth, left his combined room for the theatre. He walked timorously round about the theatre for some time. He had never been through a stage door in his life. He hoped an actor would arrive soon, under whose protection and guidance he might enter. An actor arrived and they went in together.

When you first go through a stage door there are so many notices with words like 'allowed' and 'private' and 'only' and 'warning' that you begin to wonder if you really should have come through the stage door at all. And when you first walk on to an empty stage, with its dusty floor studded with innumerable nails, and its high wall of rotten brick at the back, and its long battens above, with begrimed white, blue, or amber electric bulbs, hidden from the front by frayed borders, you can't quite abstain from reflections about the vanity of human things, the most banal reflections about sham, fifth-rate reflections upon how the most splendid presentations are at heart but dust and dirt ...

Against the wall at the back leant various flats of the scenery of 'The Coil'. In front of these several stage hands were fixing a white cloth to a large wooden frame-work. They made a thudding noise on the bare floor with their heavy boots, and they were always crying 'Right, George', or 'Let her down, boy', or something like that. Sewell was standing with his back to the fire curtain, gazing emptily at the second border. The stage manager of 'The Coil' spoke in low, conspiring tones to the electrician.

The stage manager showed Anthony his dressing-room – a bare, red-walled room with a large, low wooden shelf all round the walls, on which were three besmirched looking-glasses, one framed, one unframed, one broken triangularly. On the wall was a lively little portrait, done in grease-paint, of a girl with very black hair.

Anthony was sharing this room with another actor, Mr Gordon Dudley, who soon joined him, and whom Anthony imitated in laying out grease-paint, and powder, and cream, and covering all with a towel.

All the actors put in an appearance during the morning, and they were all cold, and could only look blankly at the stage, and say, 'What are your digs like?' or tell you what happened when they last played at this theatre. Quietly they came, hovered, and quietly scattered in couples or trios to the nearest bars.

III

Anthony had lunch at his combined room. Steak piping hot, hot plate, greasy potatoes and cabbage. And after this he lay on his bed and slept. Not sleep exactly. A worried, giddy, dim consciousness of his own cold legs, the warm pillow, the milkman's cart outside, an occasional little shriek from an opening gate, the rapping of quick heels on the pavement, coming from afar and fading abruptly around a corner ...

Tea was brought him at five and the dreary gas was lit. During tea he was for the first time really frightened about his first night on the stage. He was visibly trembling.

Walking to the theatre eased him. He found the stage

quite empty and dark, so went to his dressing-room, where he would have dressed, but was afraid that one was not supposed to dress so early.

Casually he took the lid off his powder-box, and looked at the powder, and touched it with his forefinger, and carefully put on the lid again, and took a stick of grease-paint, and dabbed streaks of colour across his palm, and arranged everything very neatly, and walked about, and went downstairs and asked the stage-door keeper the time.

The stage-door keeper gave him a letter from Diane. Anthony went back to his dressing-room happily and slowly. He was always very slow with letters from Diane.

DEAR ANTHONY,

How are you getting on? Thanks so much for your sweet letter and present. You're a dear.

I'm afraid my letter will have to be very SHORT this week as one of my *friends* is not at ALL WELL and I'm having to look after her.

I hope you'll be successful on Monday night!

Affectionately,

DIANE.

P.S. – Anthony dear, I'm not really unkind.

She had spoilt all inspiration and encouragement by the mark of exclamation after 'Monday night'. For the very first time Anthony considered the possibility of doing without Diane. He imagined little notes to her. 'The end has come at last, Diane, so I'm afraid my letter will have to be very SHORT this week – A. F.' Or 'Diane dear, I'm not really unkind, but I can't put up with this any longer. – A. F.' Or 'This is the finish, Diane. – Anthony.' Or perhaps a long, gentle, reasonable, dignified letter ending with 'I sincerely hope that you will be successful and happy, and I trust that you will realise that I am always your sincere friend, and that in any trouble you have only to call upon me. Sincerely. – A.' Or words to that effect.

He heard the voice of the stage manager downstairs. He looked at his watch. Six-thirty. At seven-thirty they rang up. He started the trembling again. Miss Robins came up the stone steps to her dressing-room, singing softly to herself. He heard her singing softly in her room until she shut her door. He heard other actors arrive, talking the faintest bit too loudly and naturally and genially to sound quite natural. Suddenly they would close their doors. There was a Battle going on behind these closed doors ... the first-night Battle.

Mr Gordon Dudley came in, asking the time, taking off coats, and starting to make up. Anthony saw that he put a little black along his eyebrows. He wondered if he ought to do the same. He tried hard to remember all that Brayne had taught him one night at the Fauconberg. He took care to bring all the colour right down into his neck, so as not to give a mask effect.

But at the end he looked nothing like Dudley. 'Is this all right?' ventured Anthony.

Dudley turned. 'Oh,' he said, 'it's a bit pale, isn't it?'

'Shall I change it?'

'Oh, no, I wouldn't change it now.' Dudley looked for matches in his overcoat.

The stage manager came clattering up the stone stairs, knocking vigorously at each door and shouting, 'Half an hour, please!'

Soon came a quiet knock at their door. The dresser. 'Oh – good,' said Dudley.

The dresser helped Anthony with the collar of his evening clothes, and did some other more or less obstructive things for both of them.

The stage manager came again. 'Quarter of an hour, please!'

Anthony said to the dresser: 'Is my make-up all right?'

'Oh, yes, sir. 'Tis all right.'

'You don't think it's too pale?'

'Ay, I was thinkin' ye were a bit pale.'

'That's what I said,' said Dudley.

'Ay, he's a shade too pale.'

'Well, shall I change it?'

'Oh, no, sir. 'Tis too late to change now.'

'There's only ten minutes more,' said Dudley.

Anthony was ready then. 'Go down and see if there are any in,' said Dudley.

On the stairs he met an actor queerly recognisable with an unexpected moustache. The actor said, 'Good luck, old boy.' He didn't seem to notice that he was too pale . . .

Brayne was on the stage, also with unexpected moustache. You were not to be in the faintest way surprised, etc ... Brayne did not seem to be nervous. He held his chin high and looked about him in a disdainful way, disdaining nervousness.

From the other side of the curtain came a low running murmur with the clank of falling seats in it and the nasal cries of 'Programme – programme' from the gallery. He peeped round the curtain. Quite a full house – all ready to believe that Anthony was an authentic actor.

The orchestra tuned. Quaint little curls and grunts of noises. A light tap, just heard, and the overture blared forth.

A certain trembling elation in Anthony while the overture lasted.

It finished. The audience clapped lightly, and murmured quietly, and shifted. All was darkness behind the set. Anthony heard the click of electric switches, and the stage manager's voice, very tense. Then the curtain rumbled up. The audience shifted, had its cough, and was very still. The first line rang out through the house.

There were ten minutes before Anthony's entrance. He waited by his door in a nervous stupor. Two stage hands were talking rather loudly near to him, and he was afraid he would not be able to hear his cue. An actor came and stood by Anthony's door and peeped cheerily through a crevice of it. 'Not a bad house,' he said. 'No, not at all bad,' said Anthony.

He heard a line which had always brought him from his

seat at rehearsals. He pulled down his coat and felt his tie. His first line was 'Hullo, where's Violet?' He would say that automatically and the rest would come all right. What *was* his second line? Oh, God, what was his second line?

He heard his cue. They were waiting for him. He fumbled with the door and opened it.

He was speaking loud and clear to a chromatic face in a mist of bright light. And the vast, populous darkness was patient, expectant, amicable.

Chapter Ten

THE PENDANT

I

Letter written to Diane from Sheffield:

DEAREST DIANE,

Thank you for your note, which I received on Monday night. You know, Diane, your heartlessness to me is really getting unbearable. Does it give you such exquisite joy to make me unhappy? Wouldn't it be just as easy and pleasant for you to give me a happy week with sleep at nights instead of misery?

Blackguardly insinuator!

And don't you realise the sort of deep relief and joy a tiny kind word from you gives me?

Oh, Diane dear, don't think I'm ungrateful, but I love you, Diane, love you, love you, love you! I feel that I must go on saying that. It gives a sort of relief.

Diane, I wonder what it feels like to be you, to be so near all that beauty. How could you ever be miserable? Of course it's simply obstinacy on your part to profess that you are not beautiful. If you are serious you are simply mad. You admit that most people admit that you are pretty. Well, the truth of the matter is this. Fifty per cent of the world would think you to be pretty, forty per cent of them would think you to be beautiful, and the remaining sensible ten per cent would know you to be beautiful.

Diane, you are such a wonderful thing of colours and harmonies and subtleties. You're like an evening sky and as cool and restful as the evening. And you are just as fresh, Diane, as early morning on a clear stream, with slim trees and wet leaves. Oh, Diane, you are beautiful.

The Poet at work.

Diane, I can never cease to love you. I don't think I want very badly to marry you. That would not only be too absurdly great a joy, but it would be a sort of sacrilege. You are the whole of life for me, now and for ever.

I simply want to worship you, near or apart from
you. All I want to know is that you do not mind my
worship and will always allow it. The only reason I
could have for wanting to marry you is in order that
no one else should do so! Because there is no one in
the world who could possibly be worthy of you.

You know, Diane, there's a sort of family
resemblance between you and all beautiful things.
Whenever I see a lovely thing in nature instinctively I
think of you and say, 'That is frightfully like Diane'.

I made my first appearance on 'the boards' last night.
The play was a simply tremendous success. The
curtain went up again and again at the end, and at
last Sewell had to make a speech. He was absolutely
wonderful. I think I did quite well and got excellent
notices (that's the name for the things the local
papers say about one). One said, 'And Mr Forster was
excellent as the young Goreham', and another, 'Good
work was put in by Mr A. Forster'.

I was not so nervous on the first night as I expected.

Time 6.30. Position: rooms in Sheffield quarter of a
mile from the theatre. Diane, I must fly.

Diane, do write a respectable letter next week. I'm
feeling simply dreadful after your last. Of course it is
sweet of you to write at all.

I should like to sit here all the night writing. I love
you, Diane. I adore you. Good-bye, dearest,

Yours ever,
ANTHONY.
P.S. – I'll let you know my address at Liverpool next week as soon as possible.

This letter started in the neatest of writing, became a bit scribbly, recovered again; and at the end the right-hand side of the lines were nearer the top of the page than the left-hand side, save the last line, which noticeably tried to improve matters.

II

In the afternoon of Wednesday Diane sat upon her bed, propped upright against her pillow, which was propped upright against the back of the bed. Her thick, bobbed hair was a little disordered; her skirt fell just above her knees, so that you just could see where the silk of the stockings ended and the coarser stuff commenced. Just beneath where the coarse stuff commenced there was the pink smudge of a little ladder. As she came to the end of each sheet she drew it away with her left hand, absently kept the hand poised for a moment, while she read the beginning of the next sheet, and then, still reading, put it behind the other sheets.

There was another bed in the room, and on this lay a tall, rather coarsely-built girl. This girl's skirt was not more than a foot from her ankles, and her stockings were all of the coarser stuff. She lay with her head at the foot of the bed, her chin propped on both sides by her palms, making two white blurs upon her chin, shown when she lifted it to turn a page of her book, or to press a page firmly down to make quite sure it would not come up again, which it always did. The book was Guy de Maupassant's stories, eighth series, translated by Bree Narran. The cover had been torn away both sides, also the advertisements. The girl was reading very quickly and skipping long passages; she seemed to be looking for something.

At last she turned over on to her back and said outright, 'Well, *I* can't see anything immoral in all this.'

'No?' said Diane, and laughed a little, and went on reading.

In the room was a small fireplace filled by a faded blue fan; over the fireplace a mantelpiece covered by green cloth; on the mantelpiece a small 'Winged Victory', a 'Fums-up', a small, grotesque brass god, other grotesques, Felix caught in one of his Jovian phases, with three pins stuck in his head, a china Spanish lady with red shawl and man-tilla, very proud, and a snapshot of a young man in white flannels. Above the mantelpiece was a coloured print of Watts' 'Hope', and on each side of it a postcard stuck to the wall with drawing pins. One of Watts' 'Sir Galahad', and the other of Burne-Jones' 'King Cophetua and the Beggar Maid'. There was a large, 'realistic' crucifix on the walls – a wooden cross and a wax bleeding Christ.

There was a double washing stand, a dressing-table

with a tray holding hair-pins, a tiny lip-stick, and a little volume of *papier poudre*. The wall-paper of the room was light. The sun streamed whitely on to a clean jug and basin. Outside could be heard the playing of tennis – the sharp hum of the ball on the racket, the noise of bouncing and little swishes, and the thin cries and laughs of girls.

Diane had read Anthony's letter many times. She had read it just after she had taken it from the rack downstairs, among the other girls. Then she had joined a group of girls talking, and noticeably turned away from the group to read it again. Then she had wandered out on to the tennis lawn with two other girls, and in tidying the hair of one of them had put Anthony's letter carefully on to the ground, and soon after had slowly wandered away, and read it. And she had been reading it on this bed for a long while now.

If she had employed words she could not have said more directly, 'I've an interesting letter here – especially interesting. Ask me who it's from and what it's about.'

And no inquiry of this nature had come yet. And after Diane's preoccupied 'No?' in face of what in usual circumstances would have been considered the almost catastrophic morality of Guy de Maupassant, it would be nothing short of an insult to withhold a question. And the girl with the coarse stockings, who had been holding out as long as she could, was constrained to appreciate this, and offered 'Who's it from this time, Diane?'

'Oh,' said Diane, in a fancy-your-mentioning-it tone, 'this is from "Anthony".'

'Is he still as passionate?' asked the agreeable, dutiful girl.
'Oh – yes.'

A pause. Now that Diane was successful she didn't quite know what to do with success. But the girl was dangerously near a return to moral Maupassant. Diane said:

'I wouldn't mind if he didn't exaggerate so terribly.'
'Oh, yes?'

Hopes for 'How does he exaggerate?' but another pause.

'For instance, listen to this,' said Diane. '"Diane, you are such a wonderful thing of colours and harmonies and subtleties. You're like an evening sky, and as cool and restful as the evening. And you are just as fre-e-esh, Diane, as early mor-or-ning on a clear stream", so on, so on, so on.' Diane blushed. 'I mean it's so silly, isn't it?'

'Oh, I don't know.'

'And then again, "I don't think I want very badly to marry you", so on, so on, so on, so on, so on, so on; "it would be a *sac*rilege." It's so absurd. Of course, he's an awfully nice chap otherwise.'

And another pause.

'Is he nice looking?'

'Well, he's got an awfully nice sort of face. I don't know that I'd call him good looking. He's got an awfully pretty mouth. I've got a photograph in that drawer there. Have a look,' said Diane, with a happy break in her voice.

The girl took three photographs out of the drawer. 'The small one's him,' said Diane. 'Not bad,' said the girl. 'He's lots better than the photograph,' said Diane.

'Who's this?' said the girl, holding out the large photograph.

'Oh, that's Jacques, another of them. He's twenty-five, by the way. But he's really lots younger than Anthony even. I always look upon Jacques as just a big baby.'

'And this?' said the girl, holding out the third.

'Oh, that's Trevor. I've told you about him.'

'And who do you like best of all these enamora?'*

'Oh, Trevor, I think. He's so rippingly unemotional. He doesn't write to me for weeks sometimes. And I know he's absolutely terribly in love.'

'Anthony's on the stage,' Diane continued, 'and he's a great friend of James Sewell, the author of "The Hungry Generations". And Gladys Busbridge. She's playing the leading part in the play he's in now.'

'What – *the* Gladys Busbridge?'

'Yes. And the awful part about it is that I believe he thinks he can make me rather jealous about Gladys Busbridge, so I have to punish him with short letters and things. It's the only way you can keep these people in order.'

Diane was twiddling a little bit of silk around her forefinger.

'I don't know that I do like Trevor best though, altogether. It's all very well to be unemotional. Anthony always proclaims—'

---

* This is the word used.

'Oh, my God, Diane. It's half-past three. I must fly. I swore I'd appear at needle-work this afternoon.'

'Oh – can't you put it off?'

'No. I really can't, dear. I'll be back about half-past four for tea.' She went.

Diane sat ruminating for a time, twiddling the bit of silk, and later polishing her nails with the right implement. Then she reached for her writing-pad and scribbled a long letter to Anthony, and put some of the most trying characteristics of Diane into it – all the uppish conceits, the half-formed, unrealised ideas, self-glorifying.

Later she wandered out into the sweet green country that lay around the school. She wandered through one or two fields sodden by last night's rain. She walked in a green path by a wood, and through the wood. She climbed a stile and went up a wooded embankment of the railway. Here she saw some old blackberries and went out of the way to pick them. (Her ankle fell into a grass-hidden little hollow and was pricked. A long twig of thorn swung out and caught her skirt with a little sound of ripping.) She ate all five old blackberries at once from her palm, and did not know that she had a purple stain at one corner of her mouth ...

She came to the top of the embankment, where there was a large, ugly warning against the trains and the converging, silver lines of the rails each side, lost at last in a haze. She heard a rattle in the grass and was in time to see a signal fall further up the line. She decided to wait and watch the train pass. Soon she thought she saw it, then saw it, then thought she heard it, then heard it. The train came nearer with ominous louder puffs. The train was a mighty roar, a tremendous clatter for a moment or two, and then a pleasing noise, fading.

When the train was beginning to lose itself in the other haze the silence hurt Diane's ears a little, and she fell to thinking about suicide by trains ...

If she died, she believed Anthony would die soon after. It was rather wonderful to think that anybody cared like that.

Jacques or Trevor would not die. They would weep, and think of her as 'little Diane', and marry later, and be happy with children.

Anthony would not weep, but die, or kill himself. So Diane thought.

She reached the bottom of the other embankment and climbed the style. A young man in farmer's gear stood the other side, giving her precedence. When she climbed over he climbed over very cleverly indeed. 'I thank you, madam', he said, displaying a manly tone, and a disposition to hover. 'Thanks', said Diane, and went on.

Anthony was rather wonderful.

The sun was getting low and rayless now. Diane went down a slope of close-cropped grass to a little brook. The brook murmured and tinkled and washed, and was sweetly smooth further up, where thick willows lazed over the water. And there was a little murmur of the brook heard above the others, soft, like a woman's tone.

Diane sat down by the brook, and opened a small volume

of Keats she had brought with her. Anthony's present. She opened it somewhere about the beginning of 'Lamia'.

> *Whither fled Lamia, now a lady bright,*
> *A full-born beauty, new and exquisite?*

And a line further down:

> *While her robes flaunted with the daffodils.*

She thought that Keats must be very lovely. She turned to the beginning of 'Endymion'. She read a little of the preface, and looked at the page opposite:

> *A thing of beauty is a joy for ever.*

That was really lovely, Diane thought. Of course! The beautiful things really did last. She looked around her and was very glad.

And she liked Anthony for giving her this book. She associated Anthony with the sweet brook, and green grass, and the daisies, and the clean pages and clear print of the book . . .

For awhile Diane thought quite lucidly. The uppish conceits, the half-formed, unrealised ideas, self-glorifying, became newly, amazingly transparent. Anthony's too. She wished that Anthony wouldn't talk an awful lot of rot about marrying her being a sacrilege, and she knew the relish it had given that afternoon.

She wished that Anthony could come to her now, and build no silly, insincere fancies around his love for her; and they might sit, without any word, by this rippling beauty. And then Anthony could take her away – not to a house where children and servants were, and meals; but to some high, sunshiny, blue place, with a calm lake and snow-topped mountains, where you didn't have to do anything earthly at all ... Where you lived for Truth, and things of beauty which were joys for ever.

You got rheumatism or something if you sat on wet grass. Diane rose suddenly and strolled back to Nunton.

Nearly home it was dark, and rather cold. Enchantment faded ... Diane became increasingly delighted by her late mood.

She imaged herself as a girl who wanders from her friends, a long way into the country, and sits down by brooks with a volume of Keats, and realises that things of beauty are joys for ever.

Tea was made for her by her companion when she reached her room.

'Where on earth did you *get* to this afternoon?' asked her companion, after tea.

'Oh, I just took a stroll miles beyond the other side of the embankment. I'm sometimes taken like that.'

'I'm going downstairs in a moment, dear. Shall I take this letter for Anthony Forster, Esquire, to be posted?'

'Would you be a dear?'

III

Anthony proceeded to Liverpool. He wandered about the Liverpool docks trying to see a liner. He found that ships were very big things. He endured much nuisance with the wind in front of Liverpool Town Hall, and thought of going to the Walker Gallery, but did not.

From Liverpool to Manchester, where 'The Coil' was marvellously well received. From Manchester to Torquay, where the small tour ended.

Anthony had a very happy week at Torquay. Happier because it was the last week, and he was looking forward to long, peaceful evenings at the Fauconberg, and the return of Diane.

Torquay he found all for love. It was a warm town, hiding in seven big hills. In the morning the hills lived against a blue sky in a green haze, and in the dusk the hills projected, monstrous and black, against the wide, fierce blue peace. There was a many-coloured sea which ran in parts right against sequestered fields, warm and hushed, with a poppy or two in them.

Anthony was in a very comfortable combined room here, save for the inappreciable perplexity brought about by the landlady's little boy, who was for ever scuffling in the passage outside just before meal-times, and suddenly, so quietly that he couldn't possibly be observed, peeping round the door, and looking at Anthony as hard as he could. The landlady was very kind, and gave Anthony the key to a chest full of books. She had to keep it locked because 'she had had ladies staying there' who 'did run off with them so'. She advised Anthony to read 'Sonia' by Stephen McKenna. 'But I haven't read it meself,' she said. 'But 'tis very good, I believe, and very successful.'

He was told by all to go to Babbacombe. Every night an actor or so said he had been to Babbacombe that afternoon. It was very beautiful.

You go to Babbacombe on the top of a tram. You climb a lot of hills on top of the tram, absently meditating upon trams falling down them again. In parts you have to see that overhanging branches of trees don't get you in the face, and you wonder why the tram company or somebody doesn't see to it.

Babbacombe *was* very beautiful. Anthony went along the high, windy cliffs, and looked far beneath him at the translucent sea, just heard. And here it was he decided he would actually ask Diane to marry him.

When he was twenty-one, he understood, he was to have an income of about eight pounds a week. On that they could be comfortable. (They only charge two pounds ten shillings per head at the Fauconberg and places like it. That's three pounds extra for enjoyments and dress.) But he was an actor now. And he would get jobs in town. Understudies and things. Not difficult. There was a dearth of juveniles. And the money he got from that would all be for extra enjoyments.

And just after marriage he would spend a little capital

for a six-months' honeymoon in Italy. And one Monday morning in Italy he would start his novel. A thick manuscript, typed at last; a book, with coloured illustrated wrapper, and deep print on thick pages ... And Fame, and money.

He was going to ask Diane, as soon as he saw her, to be engaged to him.

The wonder of marriage to her! To bring her things in bed, to serve her, and hold her hand while she talked, to call her ugly, funny names, and to be called them. To be kissed solemnly in reward for things – a lazy kiss with no pursed mouth, on the forehead. To be familiar with all the little things made magic by her association – her shoes; her bag with little mirror attached and lining torn in one place, its old letter and its two French coins; her gloves lain aside but still rather puffed out; a piece of blue ribbon hanging about for a long time, and frayed; a sometimes distinguishable grease-mark on a certain skirt ... To go to theatres at night, to come back and idly look at the programme on the bed. To sleep, his hand on her hand, and to wake at midnight for a moment to know a sweet certainty of happiness, to know their adorable little conspiracy against the whole world.

IV

One morning soon after his return to the Fauconberg Anthony was strolling along the Earl's Court Road, and he stopped for some time outside a small jeweller's shop, and imagined all the rings on Diane, and all the necklaces, and all the wrist-watches. But the best thing of all for Diane was a pendant hanging in the middle of the shop. This was nineteen pounds. Anthony passed on.

('But, Anthony dear, you shouldn't have done it. It must have cost tons. It's no use *thanking* you . . . ')

He would do it. There was a rather fascinating way of getting the money. At the Fauconberg they would charge him fifteen shillings the less if he went without his lunches. He would go without his lunches and eat bread and cheese in his room. This for two weeks and he would have enough money. He had saved a lot from the small tour.

Yes. He would sit up in his room during lunch time and eat bread and cheese. And he would read French. It was about time he learnt French well enough to read easily. He would take his difficulties to Diane . . .

So next morning, about lunch time, he went to the jeweller's shop, stayed outside the shop a minute looking at the jewel, and then, with summoned reassurance, went in.

The shop was empty. Anthony shuffled a bit. An old man came out, chewing at his lunch. 'Yessir.'

'Could I have a look at that sort of pendant thing you've got in the window – in the middle,'

'With pleasure, sir.'

'I just want to have a look,' said Anthony.

The old man, still munching, warily withdrew the pendant from the window.

'It's a very pretty little thing,' said the jeweller.

'Yes. It is rather nice. I think I'll have it then.'

'Thank you very much, sir. Let's see. Nineteen pounds, isn't it?'

'Yes, that's right,' said Anthony. And he took his left hand out of his pocket, and in his left hand were nineteen pound-notes. 'I think you'll find that's right.'

'Thank you very much, sir. Let me see, sir. I think I can find you a case for that.' 'Oh, don't trouble,' said Anthony. A little girl stumbled from the back of the shop, dealing, at the same moment, with a cheap scooter and a slab of bread and jam, listlessly with both.

'No trouble at all, sir. Dearie, just go and ask your mother if she's got one of them cases. She'll know what I mean.' The little girl went, and was heard calling 'Mummie' behind the door. The jeweller counted the notes. Then he also went, saying, 'Just a moment, sir.'

He came back with a case. 'I think this'll fit,' he said. It didn't fit at all.

'Good enough anyway,' said Anthony. 'Thanks very much.'

'It's a nice little case, you know. I'll wrap it up for you, sir.'

'Oh, thanks very much.'

'It's really quite nice and mild today, isn't it, sir?' There was an indisputable flavour of delirious joy in the jeweller's tone.

'Yes, quite,' said Anthony. 'I'll be surprised if it doesn't rain again soon though.'

'Oh, yes, we never seem to have it for long, do we, sir?'

Pendant given over to its new owner with flourish and grin.

Half-way back to the Fauconberg Anthony took the case out of his pocket. He tore the paper away. The case was rather shabby. You did not have to press the small dull button to open it. He took a little peep at the pendant. In the dull case it looked rather a second-hand, second-rate sort of thing, the sort of thing you would have found among assortments of your aunt's old stuff, never worn, and which she would have said you could have if you liked ... And then the delirium of the jeweller ...

But nineteen pounds had certainly been paid for it. Anthony didn't know anything about jewellery. A girl would know.

Anthony did not enjoy the subsequent lunchless fortnight. It is not the substance of Lunch that counts so much as the Idea. The unacknowledged goal of the morning's work is Lunch. Lunch is a post gained – a halting-place. It defines a fresh period – the afternoon. The afternoon never did start at twelve.

There was no settling down to bread and cheese. He always had this at twelve, because he was hungry and could have it. He had to hide in his room because he had told them he was lunching out. He tried to start French at the very beginning. A few exercises dwelling upon the reactions of a bewildered family to their writing material, and he gave it up. Generally he had a bath at about one o'clock.

V

Diane had arrived. At six o'clock Anthony had seen a taxi drive up. Far below, he saw her mother get out, and then herself. He could not see her face. He just heard her laugh, a little nervously, he thought. She was surely thinking of him. She went into the house and the taxi drew away. She was somewhere downstairs.

It was Saturday – a dance night at the Fauconberg. Anthony had given it out widely that he was going to dance, and he had told Betty to come.

He shaved and washed very thoroughly. It made his face rather rough and his nose red. He looked at himself many times in the glass. His hands trembled too much to fix his collar. He heard a chambermaid making noises with cans in the bath-room. He went outside and asked her to fix it for him. She had great difficulty. He stood upright looking at the ceiling while her cold hands throttled and pinched his neck.

He was ready too early. It was only five and twenty past six. He strode up and down his room with his hands in his pockets. He took out the pendant, which was wrapped now in tissue paper, and he put it in his pocket, and he took it out again.

He would give it to her on the stairs, after a dance.

He lay on his bed and listened to his heart beating.

He heard, outside the door, many running upstairs, calling amiably to each other in the passages, and he was envious of their unconcern; and then he heard the dinner gong – a pale noise, far downstairs, louder for a moment while a door opened.

He would wait ten minutes, then go straight down to the dining-room. Diane would be there, with her mother. He would go to their table, shake her hand, and say, 'Well, I'll see you afterwards'.

After seven minutes he rushed fearfully down the stairs.

Diane was not in the dining-room. He went to his little table. Soup was brought him, and he managed to get through with it. Then mutton, and baked potatoes, and cabbage – so much nasty substance wrongly in his mouth. Whenever the door opened he looked up quickly. The wrong people walked in, but they didn't know they were the wrong people.

Diane came in, followed by her mother. She was saying 'Hullo' to a few people as she passed. She sat down. He caught her in a sly, rambling glance, and said, 'Hull-o-O?' by smiling, surprised lips, and they both smiled.

They kept on smiling at each other.

When he had finished dinner he caught Diane's eyes, pointed to her plate, made a vigorous pantomime of eating, and pointed in the direction of the lounge. He went into the lounge and stood alone by the fire.

Diane, he thought, was looking wonderful. Not quite as he had expected. Not quite so beautiful perhaps. She looked almost quaintly like herself.

The evening was going to be very beautiful. He was going to recover the old tremulous excitement to the old tunes. He was going to hear her say 'Yes, Anthony', in the Diane way. She would sit out dances with him, and he would give her the jewel. Tomorrow morning he would have a walk with her, and ask her to be engaged to him.

Diane liked him a little better already, he thought. There was something in her smile.

She came out after an indifferent, hand-rubbing crowd had assembled round the fire. They shook hands amid a buzz of talk. 'How are you?' he said. 'Very well, thanks – and you?' 'Oh, I'm all right. You're looking awfully nice.' 'Oh, I'm not. I'm feeling ghastly.'

'Well, if it isn't Diane!' said a lady.

Anthony forlorn for three minutes.

'I *must* go and change my shoes,' said Diane. 'They're hurting me like anything.'

'Right you are,' said Anthony.

Desertion for ten aching minutes. She came back with a book.

'I believe the dance has started,' said Anthony. 'Shall we go on up?'

'Oh, I'm not going to dance, Anthony. I'm too tired.'

'Oh, but you must.'

'No, I can't really. I've got a headache, too.'

'Oh, have you? Oh. Can't you take an aspirin or something?' This he said in a pained voice, a very pained voice, and Diane's cute brown eyes made him want to kick himself for the very pained voice. Anthony had once said in a letter, 'To think of you in pain gives me more pain than you could ever suffer at the time.'

'Oh, yes. I might,' said Diane.

Betty ran in gesticulating. 'Mr For-or-ster – it's the third dance! You said it was with meeee! Quick. Hullo, Diane.'

'Oh, I don't feel like dancing, Betty.'

'Oh, cumm onn! Don't be an *id*yert! We'll miss it!'

'Oh, all right. Are you all right, Diane?'

'Yes – quite,' said Diane, smiling.

He was pulled away by Betty. A last glimpse of Diane opening her book.

He danced with Betty.

'You're very uncommunititive tonight,' said Betty.

'Yes – I am.'

'I know. It's Diane.'

'It's not.'

'I think she's a beast. I suppose you'll go and tell her that.'

'No, I won't.' Anthony did not quite know what was happening, or what he was saying.

He wondered what time Diane would go to bed. He dare not go down to her. It would be hanging about. He would go after four dances.

He danced another, and watched two, and could put up with it no longer. She might have gone to bed.

She was reading the book.

'Hullo, Diane. I just had to come down. Do you mind?'

'Mind? What on earth do you mean, Anthony?'

'Oh – nothing. There's nothing the matter, is there, Diane? I haven't done anything wrong, have I?'

'Wrong? Oh, of course, you're potty?'

He laughed and sat down beside her. She did not edge away . . . She made room for him.

'I've got such a frightful lot to talk about, I haven't the faintest idea where to begin. What sort of term did you have, Diane?'

'Oh, fine, thanks. Look here, Anthony, I've got a bit of a shock for you.'

'Oh, God – what's that?'

'I'm going away to France tomorrow, for the holiday.'

'Oh, no, Diane.'

'Yes, Anthony, I'm terribly sorry. I couldn't let you know before because it's only just been decided. My mother had a wire this morning.'

'Oh, Diane, this is terrible.'

'Yes, I know, Anthony.'

Anthony was almost past caring. 'Well, for heaven's sake, let's get the best out of tonight.'

'Yes, Anthony.'

'What sort of term did you have, Diane?'

'Oh! Of course, Anthony, I haven't told you. You see,

Anthony, there was a sort of competition at the end of the term for the best essay in – on Elizabethan Literature, and the girl who won it had to read her essay out to the rest of the school. I read mine out.'

'Oh! How ripping.'

'I got this.'

A deep relief to know that the book was a prize. She had brought it in to show him. She wanted him to know that she won prizes for English Literature. The book was 'Heroes and Hero-worship.'

'I always said that you could write if you only took the trouble,' said Anthony, a novelist himself. 'Do you know your "Heroes"?' 'Heroes' had a better sound than 'Heroes and Hero-worship.'

'No, I haven't read it,' said Diane. 'Is it good?'

'Oh, fine stuff. You'll like the "Mahomet" best.' 'Mahomet' had a better sound than 'The Essay on Mahomet'. 'Simply wonderful.'

He soon began to speak of Love. He said some things rehearsed, but she gave the wrong replies, and he couldn't follow them up.

Should he give her the pendant? He must give it. At every pause in their talk his heart thundered in his breast. At last, 'Diane, I have something for you.'

'Have you, Anthony; what is it?'

'Don't get excited,' said Anthony, with his voice going ever so funny, 'it's nothing much'.

Prolonged rambling in breast pocket. Withdrawal of

tissue paper. Steady interest from Diane. The pendant fell from the tissue paper on to the floor, flinging itself sportively under the armchair.

'Of course, it *would* do that,' said Anthony, on his knees.

'Oh, how sweet,' said Diane. 'Is this for me?'

'Yes, I thought it was rather pretty. But it doesn't look so nice now. Do you like it?'

'I should think I do. It's lovely. But, Anthony, it must have cost tons and tons and tons. You really are wicked.'

'Oh, rot.'

She soon said, 'Let's go up and dance.'

On the stairs she asked him to fix the pendant around her neck. He had given her a jewel, and they had to perform all the right little polite ceremonies. She had to wear it, and keep on looking at it, and be pleased. The pendant was almost a nuisance . . .

And when he had fastened it round Diane's marvellous neck, Anthony thought the pendant looked much too conspicuous, and did not look like Diane's pendant, but like a pendant Diane had put around her neck.

They stayed a few moments at the door of the ball-room, watching the dancers, and then they danced.

It was not a very sweet tune. He could think of nothing to say while they danced. He tripped once and said, 'Sorry'. She said, 'My fault.' The dance ended quickly. He tried to clap it into life again, but failed. They said, 'No good', hovered, and wandered to the door.

An aggressive young man was there. 'Hullo, Diane', he

said. 'You returned?' 'Yes, Mr Buxton, I've returned.' 'The return of the prodigal, eh?' 'Yes.' 'I observe that you are even passing beautiful as ever. We will even trip gaily the next waltz, will we not?' 'If you like.' 'How's school getting on?' 'It's not school,' said Diane, 'it's a finishing school.'

Anthony moved away, looking for somebody or other. The band started. Diane was taken away by Mr Buxton. It was one of the old tunes.

After the dance Diane and Mr Buxton came and stood by the door with many others. Anthony could just hear them.

'Hullo,' said Mr Buxton. 'What's this?' He held the pendant. 'Have you been taking a visit to Woolworth's sixpenny bazaar or something?'

'No, I have *not,*' said Diane.

'I really cannot allow this tawdry display of jewellery,' said Mr Buxton.

'I think it's jolly nice,' said Diane, rather softly. She couldn't help looking for Anthony's eyes, and she met them for one catastrophic moment. Anthony looked about for somebody, and then went to find somebody, up the stairs.

But he came down without anybody later, and found Diane dancing with a young man who had lost an arm. He had not lost his arm in the war, but people thought he had, which was just as useful for him. Anthony found Betty and danced with her. They all met in the doorway after it.

'Hullo, you've got a pendant, Diane,' said Betty.

'No,' said Diane.

'I believe Mr Forster gave it to you.'

'Mr Forster did nothing of the sort,' said Anthony.

Diane, Betty, the one-armed man and Anthony went for refreshments downstairs. Diane asked for lemonade, Betty for an ice.

The one-armed man was more successful than Anthony in the crush at the counter, because he was one-armed. He asked for two lemonades, so Anthony was left to look after the ice. He was some time in getting it. Once while Betty tied a ribbon round an ear of the one-armed man, Anthony spoke to Diane. 'I do wish I could get you alone,' said Anthony. 'I've got lots to say to you.' 'Yes, I know,' said Diane, 'but one can't in all this crowd.'

He had the following dance with her. It was one of the old tunes, and he tried to think some of the old things about her. He imagined he had a faint gleam of them for a moment, and then he held her a little firmer.

'Anthony, don't hold me quite so tight. It pulls my skirt up at the back. It's velvet.'

And he had the last dance with her.

'Diane, could you come for a walk tomorrow morning?'

'Oh, I don't know, Anthony. You see, I've got to pack.'

'Oh, Diane, please do come.'

'Oh, all right, I will.'

The band ran straight on to 'God Save the King'. Anthony was feeling rather sick. Fifteen cigarettes this evening.

'Are you going to bed now?' he asked.

'Yes, I think so.'

'Well, I think I'll get on. See you tomorrow morning. Good-night, dear.'

A hardly perceptible sharpness of glance signalled that 'dear' had been registered.

'Good-night.'

'Good-night.'

He went slowly up the many stairs to his room. Each stair spelled failure, failure, failure.

Still Diane hadn't really done anything wrong. It would be all right on the walk tomorrow.

He undressed, put on his dressing-gown, and went out into the dark passage to get hot water from the bath-room. He thought he heard a distant gramophone, and wondered.

He found his way down the many dark stairs, till he came just in sight of the ball-room.

The lights of the ball-room were low and red. The dim, hoarse gramophone was quaint after the noise and blare of the band. He heard the rhythmic shuffling of a few dancers.

Diane was among them. Her fine, erect body came round by the door for a moment. She was smiling up at her partner. She didn't wear the pendant.

Anthony went slowly up the many stairs to his room.

He flung himself on his bed, and hid his face in his hands. He could not quite weep.

The morning was fine. Anthony was full of hope. There was a dry, filthy flavour in his mouth as he came down to breakfast. She came down very late for breakfast. She didn't wear the pendant ... She was not expected to wear the pendant.

They stayed about the fire of the lounge talking with the others – sometimes a little quieter with themselves. 'Shall we be getting on, then?' said Anthony at last. 'Yes, I'll go and change and get ready.' She came back after a quarter of an hour. He was not quite sure that he liked her dress. It was a bit *too* French, damn it. It was ravishingly beautiful. He would be very proud of her as a wife. But Diane didn't seem at all easy to marry in this dress.

They set off down the sunny Square without a word. The Walk had started.

Much had to be done on this Walk. It was the last for a long time.

He didn't like to start too early. He didn't like to clamour of love the moment they were alone.

'Where are we going?' asked Diane.

'Let's go to the Park. Let's take a taxi.'

'We'll take a 'bus.'

'Bus full on top. Nearly full inside. A seat for Anthony as well as Diane. Anthony's given later to a sharp-eyed lady who was never still, but peered at the shops. A long jolting and jarring, wrathful starts and jerking stops, a smell of petrol. If Anthony stood up too much his bowler hat flattened itself against the roof, and righted itself with a flip. He smiled at Diane once, and asked her something by his lips and eyes; she didn't understand, by her eyes.

He repeated, but she still didn't understand. So they both said, 'It's no use now', by shaking heads, and smiling, and looking away, and looking to see where the 'bus had got to.

The noise of Hyde Park was silence after the 'bus. Many birds sang, a little weary of the long summer. Diane and Anthony talked about Mlle. Lenglen.

He started suddenly, according to plan.

'Diane, will you marry me?'

'No – certainly not.'

He laughed nervously. 'No – I mean it. Will you marry me?'

'No – I won't.'

A deep silence, with his sickly, facetious murmur of 'Well, that's that, isn't it?'

'Diane, you've been awfully beastly to me since you've come back.'

'I haven't, Anthony.'

'You have.'

'I haven't,' said Diane softly.

'Now where have I been beastly?' asked Diane.

'Oh, I don't know. You might have told me you were going to dance again last night.'

A glance, almost angry it seemed, from Diane. 'Well, surely one's allowed to dance.'

'Oh, yes, one's allowed to dance ... Oh, look here, Diane. I love you. Absolutely beyond all words. Do have a bit of pity, Diane. You don't know what it means to me.

You're absolutely the whole of life. Look here, Diane, am I your best friend?'

'Yes – I think so.'

'Only think?'

'No, I'm sure. There.'

'Oh, thank heaven. Diane, will you wait a bit? Let me go about thinking I've got something to live for. You don't realise what you are to me in life. I used to dream about you when I was a kid. Years before I knew you. I really did, Diane. You're absolutely everything that's beautiful to me, Diane. You don't know how I've suffered while you've been away. You say I'm your best friend. Will you wait for me? Will you look upon me as the sort of person that you might marry? Life won't be so beastly barren then.'

'All right, I will, Anthony.'

'Oh, thanks. Oh, Diane, I do love you.'

'I'm awfully sorry, Anthony.'

'Why be sorry? . . . ' They walked along the Serpentine and round the Round Pond. He tried to make a definite position. He was her Best Friend, and she was waiting, giving a fair amount of hope.

He made the position all right; but Diane, for all the walk, was the sort of Diane who told you not to hold her so firmly because it pulled her skirt up at the back. She assented, but did not reflect his mood. All the walk she gazed, a little sideways towards her parasol, on to the ground.

She was a little kinder just at the end of the walk. Then he began slipping coy 'dears' at the end of his sentences.

'Oh, Anthony, don't call me "dear".'

'Oh, all right. I'm sorry. It is rather banal, isn't it?' said Anthony, and he blushed.

She said 'Good-bye' to him at six o'clock among a host of others. Another very pretty travelling frock. A gloved hand and a little look. He went on to the steps of the Fauconberg with her. The sun was lowering and deep yellow. He watched her, with the care-free host of others, getting into a taxi. When the taxi had gone about twenty yards she looked out of the window and waved her hand. She might have been waving mostly to him.

Somebody said, 'Charming little girl.' A lady said, 'Yes, I always think Diane's a sweetly pretty child.' A man said, 'Well, Forster, you don't seem to be expiring from unrequited love quite sufficiently.' Anthony laughed. 'I expect Mr Forster's heart is elsewhere,' said the lady. 'Oh – no,' said Anthony. 'Oh – isn't it! Much laughter. A young man from the City arrived. 'Oh, Mr Bright, perhaps you've got the news,' said another lady ...

Their voices clamoured in Anthony's ears. He ran up to his room. He could hear their voices still, far below.

A street banjo-player started 'A Little Love, A Little Kiss'. Anthony stood still to listen. There came a certain peace and fulfilment ...

He felt a tear fall on to his hand, and looked at it stupidly.

The second verse commenced, swelling again to fulfilment.

He lay on his bed listening. It stopped. Soon he sobbed, and rubbed his wet eyes against the cotton pattern of the quilt. He was amazed by the child-like sounding of his sobs. He said, 'Diane, Diane, do have a little mercy!'

VI

Diane and her mother sped on to Victoria in the taxi.

Diane's mother had grimly and finally ordered that neither of the taxi windows should be opened. After some stormy French ejaculation (in England they spoke English but quarrelled in French) they were both sulking bitterly.

In the jostled silence Diane looked sideways at her mother. In this light the heavy down upon her mother's dogged lip was abnormally heavy. And the old lady's hat was almost comically askew.

'What a sight!' thought a malevolent Diane. '*What* a sight! ...'

Chapter Eleven

THE CONFLAGRATION

I

She had given him a photograph. This was taken to the nearest framers and framed in silver.

Anthony looked at his photograph, ceremonially, every evening. He tried to find new things in it – a lovely fold of the skirt, the way the hand fell softy on the velvet dress, insolence in the eyes, tenderness in the eyes. After a few minutes he would put his lips to the cold glass, wipe away the mist with his sleeve, put it on the dressing-table, take a general glance and leave the room.

At this time he laid great stress on the holiness of Diane and the extreme white purity of his love for her. He contemplated an altar, with candles, perhaps, and praying to her. The Duke of Buckingham and Anne of Austria ...

He bought two candles and one night put them on his dressing-table with the photograph between. He undressed, put on his dressing-gown, washed, even brushed his hair. Then he knelt. Diane looked with considerate speculation over his left shoulder. He buried his face in his hands. But he could think of nothing to think.

Two minutes like this, and then he looked up. Diane looked with considerate speculation over his left shoulder. He put the candles in a drawer and went to bed. Once he took his photograph to bed with him, but he could not find any comfortable positions, and was afraid of breaking the glass.

A week after Diane had gone Brayne came again to the Fauconberg, and told Anthony that 'The Coil' was going out for quite a long tour in a month's time.

The three weeks before they started rehearsing were muddled, sickly, dreary weeks for Anthony. Far too many cigarettes. No letter at all from Diane.

Anthony hung about Piccadilly a good deal. He looked at the photographs outside the theatres. He was for ever gazing listlessly at the pictures of 'The Covered Wagon'. He looked at the pipe shop at the top of the Haymarket, where there were funny clay pipes for five shillings and unusual, expensive tobaccos – tobaccos which looked as though they had been established in eighteen thirty some-thing and which people who knew bought. He saw George Robey in Piccadilly, and Victor Maclaglen, the immense man who played in 'The Glorious Adventure'. And once he was pretty sure he recognised a small man who played employers, sea-captains, lawyers and uncles for a British Film Company.

He would have a drink when the bars opened, come out invigorated, and nearly give answer to the girls and women who looked in front of them as they passed him, as though they were having their photographs taken and finding it rather fun. He didn't say the truth to himself then, and say, 'I wish I had the courage', but he said, 'No, by Jove, I'm going to keep absolutely clean because of Diane.'

II

It was at Cheltenham, the second town on the tour of 'The Coil', that Anthony had this letter from Diane:

> I am so sorry I haven't written before, Anthony, but really I've been frightfully busy.
>
> You see, I simply HAVE to play tennis all day and all night there are lots of young men who insist upon pouring a tale of love into my ear!!!! I'm really beginning to lose my beauty sleep!!
>
> Anthony, you mustn't be so frightfully miserable.
> Do brace up, old man, because I want no *softness*.
> How's the acting?
> I expect I shall be coming back to the Fauconberg

in about six weeks and staying for quite a long while. I hope you'll be there.

Yrs. DIANE.

Forgive scribble. Am writing this on the tennis court on the top of 'Le Peau de Chagrin' which you told me to read. It's a rotten book. It's rather exciting where the skin gets smaller and smaller.

He let it fall from his hand, sat up in bed, and said aloud, 'That's finished you, Mademoiselle de Mesgrigny.'

Then he went over to the fireplace, read the letter again, and looked into the white and brown ashes of last night's fire. He had no emotion at all.

'Yes, that's finished you, Mademoiselle de Mesgrigny.'

He poured out his tea, and started eating his bacon and egg.

'Mesgrigny? What a name too.

'Quite finished you.'

He cut his new bread and tried to spread cold butter upon it. It went into lumps and tore the bread.

'By God, it'll be wonderful to be free.

'This damned woman has given me margarine.

'We will write a short note to Diane. Very short, but to the point.

'I'll tear her letters up and burn them when the woman lights the fire.'

Soon his landlady came in and lit the fire.

Anthony took all Diane's letters from his trunk. A thick,

blue packet. He had not properly looked at them for a long while. He was conscious of the first reluctance. Here, in a huddled lump, lay the endeared outward signs of a long, rich summerful of new, unbelievably sweet sensations.

They took some time to burn. Then there was the photograph. That, with all the silly patience of a photograph, looked well at Anthony while the flames curled around it. Then he wrote the letter.

> Diane, your complete lack of sympathy and total want of understanding have at last broken everything. Don't trouble to write. – ANTHONY.

He took it out and posted it. He had no emotion. He tried to bring to light some sensation as he heard his letter fall softly among the other letters, but with no success.

And he was strangefully forgetful and uninterested through the day. It was a grey, windy day with a little yellow sun shining on grey, drab houses and wet streets. A milk-cart clattered about; sometimes a traction engine or a lorry would pass, uproaring and shaking the ground; sometimes a solitary cyclist in a mackintosh, his tyres hissing loudly on the wet road. The day itself was not emotionally helpful.

Chapter Twelve

DEDITIO

I

At Brighton Anthony composed a short poem about the loss of Diane, crowning the emotional crisis by throwing his poem into the sea. This was not owing to any undervaluation of his own art. In such a circumstance the waste-paper basket would have done as well. Anthony was induced to offer his poem to the waves (grey, stormy, twilit waves they were) from directly symbolic and romantic motives.

Anthony first thought of writing his poem while walking on the slippery extremities of the West Pier at evening. There was a finely suggestive sea, a violent sunset, and Anthony was all alone on those slippery extremities. He soon tumbled to his brooding isolation, and it took him next to no time to have himself a Lonely Figure communing unfathomably with all this gloomy glory ... He lowered his head and arranged his legs into the sympathetic posture, and thought of his poem.

His poem was about Diane and would be called 'Relinquishment'. Or possibly 'Surrender', or better still, a Latin paraphrase for one of those terms ... 'Deditio'. That wasn't very good, but it would do. It would be called 'Deditio'.

Before ten minutes had gone Anthony had the whole of his poem, roughly, in his mind. Anthony's poem was partly spontaneous, but some portions were merely pot-pourris of the most beautiful odd lines of Poetry he had made here and there during the last year or so. He could not, however, work in quite all of them. Anthony's poem was written in heroic blank verse with free anapæstic substitution. It was conceived in four movements.

The first movement began with a reproach to Diane, and then described a greater upheaval in the poet's personal affairs than even he had suspected formerly. The poet dwelt upon his melancholy march into the dark:

> *You have broken the faith* (went the first
>   movement), *I must go on alone.*
> *Out from the friendly lights and the friendly*
>   *faces,*
> *Out from the joyous, rhythmic dance of living,*
> *The flash of colours and the homely*
>   *laughter—*
> *Into the dark, apart and unbefriended.*

You have broken the faith. I must go on alone.

The next movement was to be the best movement. It was able to weld together, in all aptness and harmony, all those odd beautiful lines.

'And yet there'll be my friends, and you not there,' it argued.

> *My dearest one, there will be compensations.*
> *A little of you will creep along the winds,*
> *Whispering sweet of old, embalmed days*
> *With you. Some something something*
>   *something some*
> *Some some and I shall watch the stately*
>   *sunsets*
> *Some something some some something*
>   *something some*
> *Dear as the bitter sunset of your lips.*
> *And for your hair I'll have some something*
>   *some,*
> *And for your eyes some something some the*
>   *lake*
> *Hoarding the noon's warm beauty. And for*
>   *your voice*
> *The soft and intricate ripple of low bells—*

That was the line of the piece. 'The soft and intricate ripple of low bells.' 'The ripple of low bells.' Anthony could not but assent to the transcendent quality of that phrase in English Poetry. (As one of his dream-critics had once said, 'The line of Forster's, "The soft and intricate ripple of low bells", with perhaps Tennyson's "The murmuring of innumerable bees" takes its place unchallenged as the finest single line in English Literature. It is the triumph and climax of onomatopoeia. Those bells are soft enough, in truth, but more audible than from any earthly steeple.')

> *The soft and intricate ripple of low bells,*
> *Heard in the something something something*
> > *some.*

No. Heard in the twilight. No. Pealing in twilight. Pealing in twilight o'er— Pealing in twilight o'er— Pealing in twilight o'er – possibly Fiesole – pending further information of that town:

> *The soft and intricate ripple of low bells,*
> *Pealing in twilight o'er (Fiesole).*
> *All these shall be my loves ...*

That was the end of the second movement. The third movement was the shortest, briefly depicting the discomforts and terrors of a poet superannuated:

> > *... Perhaps one day,*
> *When I am old, and cold, and about to die,*

Fearing the Void with stark unholy terror,
Quivering before the darkening waste of
     Death,
I'll cry for you, my dear . . .

The last movement was slow triumphant ecstasy:

               . . . And you will come,
Not as you came of old, but kindlier,
And hand in hand together we will go,
And all that Void will be a jewelled splendour,
And peace undreamed, reflected in your eyes,
Some something some, some something
          something some,
And I shall sleep, dear, sleep . . .

And then the poet, carried away, was brought abruptly
back to the existing chilly circumstances. He gave a sar-
donic, dry laugh to Fate, threw back the poor tears in his
eyes, and added:

               But foolish me.
You have broken the faith. I must go on alone.

And that was all.

Anthony walked away towards the theatre making plans
for the disposal of his poem. He thought of sending it in
to *The Poetry Review*. He might even have to go at *The*

Spectator or *The Saturday Review*. In face of the previous reluctance of those journals . . .

But this was hardly a commercial affair, was it? No, by God, he would not give his own sacred sadness to the multitude. It would hardly be fair to himself or Diane, Anthony argued. This was the last. It was farewell. Rossetti, he remembered, at his wife's death, had interred all his poems in her grave. How could he now duplicate such an action? He might give his poem to the sea. Yes, that was plainly the next best course to take. Death absent, the sea was adequately boundless and mysterious. Yes, he would write his poem out and throw it into the sea. That would have to be tomorrow evening.

He was given the opportunity of writing out his poem at lunch time the next day. For Mr Brayne was not lunching at home, but with his cousin. Mr Brayne had no particular liking for lunching with his cousin, he explained to Anthony, but he couldn't very well refuse. One had, sometimes, to fulfil these social obligations. As a matter of fact it was a bit of good policy to keep in with this particular cousin. He was, said Mr Brayne with light deprecation, almost fabulously wealthy. Owned half the land around these parts. Twelve servants in all, Mr Brayne believed. 'One's always liable to float into a belted earl or so', he added with a dry laugh, as though *that* was rather a nuisance.

To the munch, munch, munch of his midday meal

Anthony wrote out two copies of his poem, and a fair copy.
This was the poem completed:

You have broken the faith. I must go on alone.
Out from the friendly lights and the friendly
faces,
Out from the joyous, rhythmic dance of living,
The flash of colours and the homely
laughter—
Into the dark, apart and unbefriended.
You have broken the faith. I must go on
alone.

And yet there'll be my friends and you not
there.
My dearest one, there will be compensations.
A little of you will creep along the wind,
Whispering sweet of old, embalmed days
With you. And I shall watch the stately sunsets,
Building red towers o'er lost and gleaming isles,
Dear as the bitter sunset of your lips.
And for your hair I'll have the shimmering
dusk,
Odours and scents of rarest old-world beauty.
And for your eyes the stillness of the lake
Hoarding the noon's warm beauty. And for
your voice,
The soft and intricate ripple of low bells

Pealing in twilight o'er Fiesole.
All these shall be my loves.

                    Perhaps one day,
When I am old, and cold, and about to die,
Fearing the Void with stark, unholy terror,
Quivering before the darkening waste of
                    Death,
I'll cry for you, my dear . . .

                    And you will come,
Not as you came of old, but kindlier,
And hand in hand together we will go,
And all that void will be a jewelled splendour,
And peace undreamed, reflected in your eyes,
And I shall sleep, dear, sleep . . .

                    But foolish me.
You have broken the faith. I must go on alone.

Anthony was not perfectly comfortable about his creation, even in this last form. There was that line about the
red towers . . . He hoped it wasn't implied that the towers
were as dear as the bitter sunset of Diane's lips. It was the
sunset that was that. And then in those last lines, if you
were striding proudly down the jewelled regions hand
in hand with Diane, how came it that you went to sleep?
The recumbent phases had been almost calamitously

omitted. Anthony was indeed very anxious that his poem should be lucid in every particular, if only for the English Channel's benefit.

After lunch he put the poem away and rested in the armchair. The beer had been heavy and the fire was hot. Deciding to dispose of his poem directly after tea he went into a deep sleep.

He awoke at half-past four. The fire was black and grey, and colder than any cold thing. There was a heavy wind rising, and the rain made his window one sombre sheet of moving water, and all was tingling silence in the house. The silence was indeed so awesome as to make Anthony fearful of breaking it by asking for his tea. But at last he staggered to the door and out into the passage. 'Mrs Gillrake', he cried amiably at the top of the basement stairs. 'Mrs Gillrake'. And then 'Mrs Gillrake?' he called, gently questioning. Mrs Gillrake came creaking and breathless to him. 'Do you think I could have a little tea?' asked Anthony.

It was a quarter of an hour before she brought the tea, and Anthony was afraid it would soon be too dark for his ceremony of dedication.

He drank his tea in gulps. He folded his poem four times and placed it carefully in an inside pocket with some of last Friday's salary. Then he removed it to another pocket, as it would not do to confuse the papers in the coming windy ceremony. He left the house.

The wind yelled and the rain stung his face, but he made an unfaltering, matter-of-fact way to the sea. He should now recapture the Mood. He was somehow reluctant and unconfident. He would wait till he reached the sea.

On the whole it would be best to alter the mood from that of last night. It was really too dark and windy for the old mood. You couldn't stand, brooding and Dantesque, on a promontory, with a night like this. Plainly the mood would have to be changed to something about sea-spume flying, and thunderous dark seas, and great winds. That was right. A great wind from the sea to blow his love away. Yes, that was very good. He would stand on the farthest, most dangerous edge of the West Pier (it wasn't really dangerous, by the way, was it?) in the fury of the elements. He would look rather like that portrait of Byron. His hair would soon become dishevelled into a care-free wildness, as in that portrait, and his tie would be flapping, also as in the portrait. Anthony at once undid his tie and turned it into something that would flap better. Then he came to the West Pier.

He had no small change. Now it seemed foolish to Anthony to offer a pound to be changed to go on the pier in such weather-weather fit only for the most actively romantic pier-walkers. Moreover, he noticed that That Girl was in charge of the turnstile, that rather pretty girl rather like Diane, who had spotted him so ruthlessly in a prolonged side-long stare yesterday morning. No, the pier was out of the question tonight. He went down the stone steps towards the beach, and thus came at once face to face with the necessity of creating his mood.

Well, this was the last, thought Anthony; this was the last. The great sea and wind would gather the last memory of those splendid days with her ...

The emotion was not coming too well. He reached the edge of the beach and struck last night's attitude.

This was the end, thought Anthony, and this was the end.

He took the neatly-folded poem from his waistcoat pocket. He must wrap it round a stone. He did that and struck his attitude again. There was no use delaying the moment. Should he throw with an over-hand or a lob? A lob. 'Well,' said Anthony, 'this is the last,' and he paused. 'The last, the last. Farewell, Diane, farewell.' He thrust his poem with a gesture as black and despairing as possible into the sea.

The sea, however, rejected the timid offer, and with an air of quick finality, snatched the poem away from the stone, and sent it flying up to a far bank of the beach. 'Oh, damn,' said Anthony, chasing it. But it dashed away and away from him.

He did recapture it, came down to the sea's edge again and endeavoured to recompose himself. He wrapped his poem well round a smaller stone, and this time, with little valedictory talk, offered it again.

The sea accepted it this time, but was indifferent almost to the point of absolute unconsciousness.

Did you walk away now, or do some more motionless brooding? The sea decided that by putting forth a disrespectful frothy tongue to an unaware Anthony, and soaking his boots.

'Oh, curse!' said Anthony, and again tried to compose himself. Something had to be thought. It was out of the question to go away and forget about Diane after such bathos.

He tried the hollow laugh of disillusionment. 'Take her, great sea,' he said, possibly alluding to Diane. And the sea, more waggish now than indifferent, thrust out another white tongue, as though to say, 'Get away with you'.

Anthony left the beach and began to walk homeward. 'And now I'm never going to think about her again,' he said. The front was almost deserted. The high, pallid lamps were flickering unsteadily all the way along on to the shining wet pavements. He passed a sea-gazing young lady in a mackintosh, who was obviously another practical romanticist like himself. She seemed to stare at him and he remembered the picturesque arrangement of his tie. He passed a grocer's boy fighting the wind by standing up on the pedals of his creaking bicycle. Anthony felt cold, turned his coat collar up, and was oppressed by the invincible, indifferent actuality of his surroundings. He saw the warm, pink lights from the great lower windows of the hotel on his left, and a little further on he came across a blind paper man, head thrown back, stamping his feet, and crying 'Paper – paper' to the wind.

II

Next morning Anthony bought yet another exercise book. On the first page he wrote 'Miscellaneous' and on the second page he copied his poem of relinquishment to Diane, ever so neatly.

III

At most of the towns Anthony lodged with Mr Brayne. Mr Brayne was the best person to lodge with. There was no quaking before the landlady with Mr Brayne. When Mr Brayne wanted more coal Mr Brayne went to the top of the stairs and asked for more coal. And when he wanted hot water at any quaint time he asked for it. And he asked for a kettle at nights with which to fill his hot-water bottle, and if it wasn't there he asked for it. And he bought most of the food, and would always severely audit, if not actually dispute, his landlady's bill at the end of the week. And Anthony benefited by all this.

Of a night, after the show, the two would build themselves a high fire in their sitting-room. Mr Brayne would lie in the armchair; Anthony would sit in a small chair right over the fire, and find soft parts of the coal with a poker, and prod them while they talked.

They talked until the high fire was old and grey and cold, until the clock on the mantelpiece had sung out two startling little notes, and still they talked, shirking their colder rooms. Mr Brayne did most of the talking. He lay right back in his chair, infatuated with new-discovered worldly wisdom, and summed things up for Anthony.

One night they talked of Love. Mr Brayne put the whole thing in a nutshell for Anthony. 'The human animal,' said Mr Brayne, 'has a natural desire to mate with a member of the opposite sex.' There was nothing else to be said after that!

At about a quarter-past two all would be a dull dream in the dull green light of the loud-breathing gas. Then Mr Brayne and Anthony would yawn and stretch themselves to their fullest extent. Out went the light. They would mumble a few things and 'Goodnight' and trip up the black stairs and passages to their rooms.

In his room Anthony would wake again. He would wash in water biting cold, and get tremblingly into the big double bed. He would take his last Gold Flake, specially reserved, and smoke it, looking at the gas.

And then nearly always, about half-way through the Gold Flake, he would get out of bed and go to his coat, which hung over a chair, take a slip of paper from it, get into bed.

It was the piece of paper on which Diane had written the words about cheering up, and the stiff, black starfishes. Anthony had found it in his pocket a long while after the great conflagration. The words were smeared now, and shiny, and faded.

Anthony would just look at this.

But when the light was out, and Anthony was comfortable and not at all tired, he started all the old organised Thinks. Sometimes he thought about his stirring life after some great, eventual Monday, but usually he thought about Diane. He thought most extravagantly about Diane.

There was a war, Anthony would think, for instance, with America or something like that. Only there wasn't conscription and not many men joined up. But it was a terrible war and absolutely everybody's life was threatened, only *somehow* only very few men joined up. They were looked upon as the salt of the earth. They were the real old kind of heroes, in fact. The newspapers did nothing but talk about them, and praise them, and women wept about them. To be one of them was to be the most talked-about person, the most adored person, the most stared-at person in the street . . .

They were recognised in the street because they wore a special uniform. It was a blue-grey uniform of the finest material – foreignified, with slack trousers finely creased, gold business about the shoulders, a high collar, a fine wide, brown belt, and a neat sword . . .

Anthony turned up in this dress at the Fauconberg Hotel. Everybody simply stared at him, but he was frightfully nice to everybody, and natural, and humble, and all that, just as though he wasn't one of the salt of the earth . . .

It was a dance night, and he danced all the evening with Diane. She simply didn't know what to say to him. They didn't talk about love, He stayed at the Fauconberg for the night, and went off to the war with America very early next morning. Diane was there. (She hadn't slept all night.) Anthony said to her, 'I know that I'll never come back. I've loved you always. I shall love you as I die. Good-bye.' And he gave her one soft kiss in the light of the early morning, and went ...

In the war with America he became absolutely the salt of those who were the salt of the earth. By an act of scarcely imaginable bravery, and endurance, and courage he ended the whole war. He was *lit*erally carried through the streets on his return. He was loved and adored by all. (He was in his blue-grey uniform.) He could have married any queen, but he married Diane ... ('Diane de Mesgrigny's the name,' he said to the reporter, 'if she'll have anything to do with me.')

Or before he went to the war with America, he was staying at the Fauconberg and there was rioting in the streets of Earl's Court. The people who were rioting were sacking all the houses in Earl's Court. The people in the hotel were in a panic. Anthony in firm, unpanicky, quiet tones (in his blue-grey uniform, too) ordered them all about and kept order, and they looked to him. Then he brought out his revolver. (He had a revolver – a big, silver thing in a neat leather case on his hip.) He produced his revolver and stood at the window, firing. A bullet hit his head, bringing blood, but he didn't flinch. Diane was in the offing ...

Then his cartridges gave out. So he took his sword and

went down to the steps of the Fauconberg, and engaged in a duel with a man there. As a matter of fact this man was the leader of the rioters. And he was the first swordsman in Europe. It was a wonderful duel with all those neat parries, and thrusts, and dodges, and funny gestures and feints which you see in expert fencing. Diane was in the offing. Anthony won the duel ... (Halfway through the duel the sword of the first swordsman in Europe went flying up into the air. Anthony caught it, threw his own sword dexterously and chivalrously to his opponent, and went on with the duel.)

And so on. Of course, Anthony was getting on for sleep when he thought like this.

Sometimes he simply dreamed that he was back at the Fauconberg, and Diane told him that she loved him, and they danced the last dance together, and took a long walk after it.

Chapter Thirteen

THE TRAVELLERS

I

The tour continued for twenty weeks, and Anthony was given a much larger part with a much larger salary, to the undeniable elevation of Mr Brayne's chin. Ten pounds a week he was given, and he saved a hundred pounds. Mr Brayne had saved even more. They returned to the Fauconberg well contented.

And then Mr Brayne received a legacy of three hundred pounds from his uncle. Mr Brayne had lost his uncle, of course, and so his emotions were mixed – but not well mixed. He brought the news to Anthony one morning, and when Anthony had done with his grave applause, made the most startling suggestion.

'I'm thinking of having a week in Paris,' he said. 'What'd you say to joining me?'

'I say, that's rather an idea,' said Anthony.

'It's rather an idea.'

'I don't know if you feel you can afford it. I was thinking of doing the thing more or less in style. Staying at the best hotels, and all that sort of thing. I feel I can allow myself a treat. It wouldn't be so very expensive. The exchange is very good.'

'It's a distinct Idea,' Anthony replied. 'It's a distinct Idea. But should we get on all right? Have you ever been to France?'

'Oh, yes,' said Mr Brayne. 'I was there a few years ago with my people.'

'What I mean is, I can't speak a word of the language. Would we be able to get on all right?'

'Oh, yes,' said Mr Brayne; 'I can speak enough French to carry one through. I don't mind taking charge of all that part of it.'

'Well, if you can do that I should simply love to come. How much did you say about it would come to?'

'Well, that's the point. If we stay at the hotel I have in mind, and allowing for money to enjoy ourselves properly with, I should say about forty pounds. At the outside.'

'And that includes fares, and all that?'

'Oh, yes.'

'Well, that's all right. I can do that. Well, it's on then. When shall we start?'

'I'll go and fix it up at Cook's this afternoon. I expect it'll be in about three days.'

Soon after Anthony went up to his room, and paced up and down it for more than half an hour.

Paris. What high adventure! To cross the sea and walk upon the great mainland of Europe! Actual Paris! It had never been an actual city to Anthony – just a hearsay city, as unreal as ancient Carthage. The Bastille. The Revolution. Versailles. Zola's Paris and Du Maurier's! He would spend the whole hundred pounds on the trip if necessary. He would go to Fontainebleu. All day in the quiet forest planning his novel. He would sip something or other at cafes, watching the gay crowd, and all that. There would be lots of stuff for a novelist . . .

'*I* was in Paris not long ago,' he would say to Diane . . .

The same evening Anthony sat with a book on his knees gazing into the lounge fire. An old lady – a quick knitter – sat near to him. They had been talking about the variation in the 'bus fare for a journey from the top of Earl's Court Road to the Lion Gate, Kew Gardens, and now there was a pause.

'Hasn't the weather been dreadful lately?' remarked Anthony.

'Yes. Hasn't it? It was warmer tonight though, wasn't it? I think we'll be having it better now.'

'I hope so,' said Anthony.' For myself.

'I'm off to Paris in three days,' he added.

'Oh, really? That must be very nice.'

'M'm,' replied Anthony, gave a tiny laugh, looked into the fire, and continued reading.

Manifestly the young man was a hardened excursionist.

II

They took an early train from Victoria to Folkestone. Mr Brayne managed everything and Anthony was meek. Mr Brayne tipped accurate threepennies, sixpences, and one magnificent shilling. He never looked at the objects of his largess, but considered the horizon while the money dropped from him unaware into an alert palm. When all was in order he took Anthony into the refreshment-room, where each had a poached egg on toast and a cup of Bovril. During all these arrangements Mr Brayne's chin remained at a steady angle of about a hundred degrees with his neck – perhaps rising to a hundred and ten when he tipped. Throughout the whole trip Mr Brayne's chin served as a perfect natural thermometer recording accurately the waves of Mr Brayne's embarrassment, self-defence or hauteur.

They reached Folkestone easily. As they made for the boat they saw the muddy sea undulating roughly and streaked with foam. There was a strong wind blowing, and a thin rain. 'So much the better,' thought Anthony. 'I'll stand right at the prow, facing the fine wrath.' 'Are you a good sailor?' he asked of Brayne. 'Oh, yes,' said Brayne, 'I'm never sick going across a small way like this.' 'I don't think I shall be either,' said Anthony. 'I think it's all more or less brought on by auto-suggestion.'

They reached the boat and Brayne procured a cabin. He ordered two brandies and soda. 'That's the best thing you can take,' he said.

The boat started while they were still standing nervously alert in the cabin. 'What are you going to do?' Anthony asked Brayne, 'because I think I'll be going up on to the deck.' 'Oh, I think I'll get a chair down here, and read,' said Mr Brayne, but immediately lost the point by falling over the table. 'You have to be careful of these damn lurches,' said Mr Brayne.

Anthony made for the upper deck by zigzag small excursions, dives, and breathless halts. He stood at the prow for a little while. It was a truly noble sensation. You felt like a sort of God. Nevertheless Anthony did not remain at the prow for a prolonged period . . .

Moved by curiosity, he came below again. Mr Brayne was reading in a chair. He smiled at Anthony. Anthony went and had a look at the smoking-room, and thought how jolly it was, and he had a general look-round the ship. Then he thought it would be better to be up on the deck, in the fresh air. He went up on the deck.

He shouldn't have stood at the prow like that. It was well known that the prow was the worst place to stand at.

There were various sorts of bad sailors, he knew. The

sort who felt a bit sick, the sort who felt sick, and the sort who were sick. Now Anthony was certainly not going to be sick . . .

He would stay upon the deck.

He went below. Mr Brayne was no longer in his chair. He was lying down in the cabin.

'It's come on,' said Mr Brayne.

'I'm feeling damned awful myself,' said Anthony. He looked about him with a gaze at once wild and sinisterly level.

'They're under the seat,' laboured Mr Brayne.

After fifteen minutes Anthony raised himself a little and resolved that this could go on no longer.

He must ring the bell. The boat must be stopped. Some power had to intervene. A man can't be allowed to die.

Then he lay down again.

The steward came in and arranged their cushions. 'That's quite all right. You'll be all right. Do you more good than harm. You'll be quite all right,' said the steward, and went out.

III

Messrs Brayne and Forster made an undistinguished landing at Boulogne. It was raining. They stumbled and mumbled through the Customs and boarded the train for

Paris. They found their reserved seats and did not speak. Immediately after the train started they were summoned vigorously to the first lunch, and they went.

The time was inexorably approaching when Mr Brayne would be constrained to exercise that French of his. Mr Brayne's chin shot up to a hundred and ten; he frowned but was unconcerned.

'I don't feel much like lunch,' said Anthony.

'Oh, I expect you'll be able to manage something,' said Mr Brayne, thoughtfully.

An attendant came and clattered some plates in front of them. Then another attendant came, holding a large plateful of fish, and he spoke to them in his own language. 'Oui,' said Mr Brayne, 'oui.' For that they were given fish.

'It's no good,' said Anthony. 'I can't eat it. I think the best thing I could have'd be a little brandy.'

'Oh, very well then. I'll order it for you.' Mr Brayne's meal was suspended while he waited to pounce on the opportunity. 'Er—' he said to the whirlwind attendant. 'Er— Koanyak, s'il vous plaît?'

'Brarndee?' asked the attendant. 'Brarndee arnd soadwotter?'

'Oui,' said Mr Brayne, and Anthony said 'Oui' too.

'Merci,' said Mr Brayne, when it came.

At 16.30, as Mr Brayne called it, they reached Paris. A faded blue porter attended to them. They went through some more Customs for their registered luggage. Then

'Tacksee?' asked the blue porter. 'Oui. L'auto,' replied Mr Brayne.

Theirs was a great hotel near the Place de l'Opera. 'We'll go to the Opera,' said Mr Brayne. 'These foreigners are wonderful at that sort of thing. I wonder which one they're doing.' Then they drove up to the hotel.

It was a great hotel indeed. It could take you two minutes to walk from one end straight to the other. The hushed, inimically luxuriant ground floor comprised the hall, the lounge, the dining-room, the winter garden, and the restaurant. The true light of day was never in these. All was rosy soft light, ardent red shade and the keen blaze of jewels in great glass cabinets. The air was warmly palpable, redolent of the restaurant and cigar smoke, clouds of which remained inertly spreading and curling into well-considered shapes. No voice was ever raised in here, and the sounds were as uniform as the light and the atmosphere. The lift clicked and rose noiselessly all day long. Shoes rapped smartly on the white marble floor, and all at once were whispering and creaking on the deep carpet: there was the low flow of conversation, and the steady dead murmur from the two revolving doors. This was the hotel – this ground floor. The other five floors were remote, forgotten regions of informal servants and grey utility.

They were shown to their room on the fourth floor. Their rooms were adjoining, and by opening two doors you could get from one room to the other. Anthony came into

Mr Brayne's room and sat in the armchair, dully wondering if it was a happy thought to have come to Paris.

'Well, what about some tea?' said Mr Brayne.

'Yes – rather. What does one do?'

'Oh, I'll order it by the 'phone.' He went to the 'phone. There was a pregnant silence.

'Thé pour deux, et des gateaux,' ordered Mr Brayne, all at once. 'Oui ... Oui ... Pour deux ... Oui ... Merci.'

That was all. The chin jumped up to a hundred and twenty. Whistling faintly, Mr Brayne strolled to the window. 'God, I hope it's not going to rain all the time we're here,' he said.

Tea was brought, as everything else was brought at this hotel, fussily, with some light hovering for a premature gratuity.

'I think I'll have a bath,' said Anthony after tea. 'What does one do?' 'Oh, you'd better 'phone for the valet.' 'What does one say?' 'Oh. "Le valet, s'il vous plaît", 'ld do well enough. You'd better ring from your room or they'll come to mine.'

Anthony went into his room, paced up and down his room, and at last dashed to take off the receiver.

Tickett. Lackitt ... 'Oui, monsieur.' 'Er. Le valet, s'il vous plaît?' French. Resolute and relentless. 'Oh. I don't know. I want a bath.'

'Oh, oui, monsieur.'

Soon there was a knock at his door.

'Entrez,' said Anthony, and then, 'Come on.'

It was a chambermaid.

'Parlez-vous Anglais?' asked Anthony.

She delivered a statement more reproachful than stern, still in the same beastly language.

'Well. You see. Je ne parle pas Anglais.'

That was taken in silence, being neither here nor there to the chambermaid.

'I want a bath.'

'Oui, un bain, monsieur.'

'Oui, un bain.'

French eager, comprising the words 'savon', 'frapperai', and 'trois minutes.'

And sure enough in three minutes she knocked for him and took him to the bath-room.

At seven they went down to dinner. Even Mr Brayne was confused when faced by that enigmatic menu and the stone-wall expectancy of the waiter. But at last, 'We'll start with soup, anyway', said Mr Brayne, and the waiter began to make tepid suggestions. There could have been no happier suggestions, thought Mr Brayne and Anthony.

They had to pay for their dinner then and there. It came to a hundred and two francs. 'You'd better give me your share,' said Mr Brayne, 'and I'll pay it.' Finding the exact share was a muddling business. They were as exact as possible, but with the most gallant depreciation of each other's expenditure. Mr Brayne won honourably by six francs.

After dinner they decided to go to a cinema, and as it was

raining, took a taxi there. The chin remained at a steady level and all repose was maintained until the encounter with the woman who showed them to their seats. That done, she placed the lit torch between their shoulders and remained perfectly immovable. 'Pour la service', she said at last, without intonation. Anthony gave her five francs, for which she seemed very grateful. It was an American film showing – a Larry Semon Comedy. The sub-titles were in French, necessarily, and that language did not fairly render the unreserved colloquialism of the English words. After the comedy the screen was raised, and there were some performing parrots, who also somehow managed to do their work in French. Then there was a news film. And then a girl came and sang a few songs. And then there was a long French film. Mr Brayne brought Anthony away before the end.

They had a long talk in Mr Brayne's room before going to sleep.

It was raining the next morning. Anthony went into Mr Brayne's room, and after some sleepy greetings Mr Brayne ordered 'Café complet' for two. By degrees they dressed, and went downstairs. It was impossible to go out in such rain. Mr Brayne bought some newspapers, they went into the winter garden and had liqueurs. They spoke very little. Anthony read the *Daily Mail*, but Mr Brayne read *L'Echo de Paris*. And then *Le Matin*. 'Have you got this speech of Baldwin's in your paper?' he asked Anthony. 'Very good.'

They had a light lunch and were able to take a stroll in the afternoon. A dull walk in a greasy Paris. Anthony's mind was stagnant, forever lazily reverting, for no reason at all, to the word 'blanchisseuse'. It ran in his head as a silly tune sometimes will. They finished at the Louvre, where they did hundreds of pictures.

Mr Brayne was all for the Opera that night, but on inquiry they found the Opera was closed. 'Oh, that's a damn shame,' said Anthony. 'It puts an end to that.'

They decided to go to a music hall. Mr Brayne did not actually desire to look in at the music hall for the sake of the music hall itself. But, 'It's one of those places it's well to have *seen*,' he said.

On arrival there, with a poignant memory of last night's catastrophe, Anthony's tipping was given its head. He tipped the taxi-man, he tipped the man who opened and shut the taxi door, he tipped the man who showed him where the box office was, he tipped the man who showed him where to go to get his tickets numbered, he tipped the man who sold him a programme, and he tipped, and tipped, and tipped.

The show commenced with a large chorus, dressed. There followed three more scenes with little improvement. But just before the fourth scene one or two English and American ladies and gentlemen were seen to be withdrawing. Very absently and tolerantly they retired, but in their eyes there was no mistaking the gleam of almost greedy self-approbation. The men were, in Mr Brayne's phrase, taking their Women out ... He would have given much to be able to take his Women out, too.

It was a disappointment, really. It was all done in a setting of frothy white cascades and green weeds. These were Nymphs. A very different thing. Nymphs and a bathing Diana are one thing, and undressed twentieth-century chorus-girls are another ...

After many more songs and scenes the interval came.

'Let's take a little stroll,' said Mr Brayne.

They went into the large hall in front of the theatre, where another band was playing. Anthony soon became aware that the revue itself was but incidental in the schedule of the evening. And then Anthony noticed, and Mr Brayne noticed too, that Things were Happening.

'This of course,' said Mr Brayne, 'is seeing life with a vengeance.'

A talkative girl in brown attached herself to Anthony, pleading with him. A girl in black did the same to Mr Brayne. And the two ladies walked along with them like importunate London flower sellers.

There was nothing to equal the elated and awful confusion of Anthony and Mr Brayne!

The crisis passed.

'Not tonight I think,' said Mr Brayne, plainly amused.

With ostentatious leisure they scurried back to their seats.

Surely that chin would never be down again!

In the second half of the show, however, the stalls were far from being the same peaceful havens from the gay pageant. You were pelted indomitably by incessant rains of balloons, bananas, chocolates, dolls and other such heavy souvenirs. During the storms you kept your hand raised from motives rather precautionary than collecting. Moreover, there were frequent breathless invasions of the stalls by all but the entire company. That sort of thing was most disturbing to Anthony, but Mr Brayne was amusedly susceptible. Indeed, when towards the end they came round on a match-saving tour with walking-stick cigarette-lighters, Mr Brayne was observed with horror to be fumbling for a cigarette. What is more, he found it in good time, flourished it doggedly, and had it lit for him. The operation was unusually prolonged owing to the excessive trembling of Mr Brayne's hand. The amiable girl, leaning over, smiled patiently. Mr Brayne trembled and *could* not light his cigarette . . .

These things have to be done.

In the hotel that night Anthony was eager for another long talk, but Mr Brayne was going to read. They had their first open squabble about it. 'You're always reading', said Anthony, with a poor attempt at a laugh. 'Oh! Am I?' said Mr Brayne, courteously unconcerned. 'Yes', replied Anthony, and left him without 'Good-night'.

Anthony decided to go straight to bed and to sleep. He went to bed, but soon learnt that the oysters, the omelette, the wine, the veal, the caviar, the cream ice and the coffee would not readily embrace the offer of sleep – those gay ingredients having appointed some small-hour revelry of their own.

For five hours Anthony lay turning and shifting in his bed, making fresh cool starts, moaning at fresh disappointments, wondering why, in particular, he had come to Paris, and what, in general, he was doing with his life.

He lay listening to the hard bustle of the traffic below, and the incessant abrupt squeal of the motor-horns, so different from the musical horns of London.

All was wrong with his mode of living, he decided. Where was that easy drama of Life that he had planned? Where was that fiery first act, Youth? He was still fooling about in the jumpy prologue. He saw that he had never begun Life. He had been content with little contests and conquests, little longings and failures ...

Anthony dwelt relentlessly upon his own shortcomings. Nevertheless there was no actual misgiving. For Anthony had no authentic belief whatever in his own shortcomings. In fact he amassed them against himself for the plain purpose of giving fuller flavour and power to the reposeful confidence of the subsequent new Resolution.

So in the dark, feeble hours of the morning Anthony pulled himself to pieces, and that done conscientiously erected something of himself more handsome and sturdy than he had ever erected. Though he decided not to employ that erection until he had returned from Paris.

In short, Anthony resolved to start Life on the Monday after the day he reached London. And this was no ordinary resolution, forgotten or broken in a day. It was starting Life.

On that Anthony turned over and tried to go to sleep, but could not.

He switched on the light and for some time endeavoured to read *La Vie Parisienne*. But he could only understand the pictures. He tried to sleep again. He had no success at all, and lay on his back and dreamed some more dashing military exploits before a highly susceptible Diane.

And then he saw that dawn was coming. Paris at dawn! He must not miss that. The dawn of a new life, and all that, as well. It was true that a dawn would be more aptly contemplated next Monday, but here was a dawn to be had for no trouble, and any dawn was better than none.

He waited until the sun had actually risen, then crept out of bed; slipped on his best trousers, his overcoat, and went out on to the balcony.

It had been raining softly in the night. To the west the pink, huddled houses on a steep incline lay in spellbound wet stillness before the ruddy light of the cold sun. One high window flamed a hard light back again. And beneath, the mauve city ... A man's shout echoed from somewhere through the grave, great streets. The stillness broke with the crisp rattle of a cart passing.

Life was to be ardent and glorious.

IV

Anthony replied to Mr Brayne's aloofness of the night before by spending most of the next day upon his bed, and after that they bickered pretty frequently for the rest of the holiday.

It was not a happy holiday. They did Versailles, and they did Fontainebleau, and some more of the Louvre. They went to another music hall, to a cinema, to the Coq d'Or, and for love of loving music spent three stifling hours attending to 'Werther' at the Opera Comique.

And one morning at seven they took a taxi from the hotel to the station, and went back home again. The magnificent hotel, beginning its day, hardly noticed they had gone.

V

On arriving at the Fauconberg Anthony and Brayne found letters waiting for them to the effect that another little tour of four weeks commenced for 'The Coil' the week after next.

And then Anthony learnt from the hotel attendant that in three weeks' time Diane and her mother were returning to the Fauconberg.

She would be here when he returned.

Of course, it put an end to that idea of starting life. For the present . . .

Chapter Fourteen

DIANE, ANTHONY, RAMON
AND MERCEDES

I

It was on the evening of Christmas Eve that Anthony
returned to the Fauconberg after his month's journey.

The people of the Fauconberg had all just gone into
the dining-room for the biggest Dinner of the year.
During this Dinner there were small speeches, clapping,
and three cheers for Mrs Egerton, who had given the
Dinner. There were crackers and wine, some streamers
shot across the room, a great mumbling noise and the
very loud laughing voice of a Mr Kingston. A turmoil of
not very funny fun.

Anthony was shown to his old room, where he did a little
unpacking; then he came down to the lounge and talked

to the hotel attendant, who told him, with the air of one in possession of inside information, that Diane was at the Fauconberg and now in the dining-room.

Just a door divided the dining-room from the lounge, and Anthony could hear all the noise – a deafening noise when the door opened for someone to come out, and quieter than ever when it shut.

It seemed as though they would never come. Anthony talked, with some hysteria, to the hotel attendant about yesterday's racing.

At last they came, blowing squeaking paper things which flung themselves out and shrivelled. They were chasing each other, catching each other, knocking balloons and things into each other's faces. While some walked a little sedately – a sedateness which Mrs Egerton's Christmas Eve dinners could confer.

And all wore fancy dresses. They were like Mr Brayne with their fancy dresses. You were not to be in the faintest way surprised, etc. . . . They had all agreed that Mr Kingston's fancy dress was the best.

In the crush and noise Anthony was talking to Diane. They were saying something about her looking well, her looking thinner, her rotten fancy dress, her fancy dress not being rotten, her fancy dress belonging to her cousin, the awful noise, her going to change into evening dress . . .

She left him, and he was talking to a young South American for whom he had once made out a Course of English Literature. The South American could not speak

English well. He contended, and took his time. 'I have redder – most of thoser – books you told me,' he said. 'Oh, yes? Did you like them?' said Anthony, thinking of Diane. 'Oh, yes. I liked them. Ier – have latelee been reed-inger – Beerrnardshaw. I thinker . . . (All this missed because of Diane) . . . butter – hee ees veree wittee.' 'Oh, yes, he is that,' said Anthony, thinking of Diane. 'Ah, hee ees.' Diane thoughts. 'Did you read any of those other books?' asked Anthony, trying to pull himself together. The South American looked at him earnestly. 'You know, those *other* books,' said Anthony. 'The Arnold Bennetts etcetera . . .'

Diane soon came back.

'Well, are we going to dance?' asked Anthony.

'Yes – rather.'

'Then shall we go on up?'

'Yes.'

Nothing said on the stairs. She went ahead of him and someone spoke to her, But just before reaching the ball-room she fell back to him.

'I'm going to get married soon, Anthony.'

'Diane, this is weird. So am I.'

He had arranged to say, after a few dances, 'You know, Diane, it's an awful shame, because we really could have been so happy together', and that was to have led to a beautiful conversation.

But she really was going to be married, it seemed. It was

a Spaniard, she told him, named Ramon, whom she had met in France. In a month's time he was coming to fetch her to America, where he lived. He had a wonderful house in a place called Tarrytown, just about twenty-five miles outside New York. She had seen pictures of it. And she really did love him. 'Yes, quite sure, Anthony.'

But Anthony did not quite succumb. At the end of their third dance he said, 'Do you think we could have been happy if we married, Diane?'

'Oh, I don't know; we might,' said Diane, tolerably softly and propitiating.

'Do you think you could have ever given me what I wanted?'

'Oh, I don't know ...' Diane's eyes were straying, and Anthony followed them intently. They lit into a smile. 'Where did you get to after dinner? I've been looking for you, Mrs Mackintosh,' said Diane, and walked to Mrs Mackintosh.

'Diane, may we sit out this dance? I've got something to tell you rather important.'

'Yes, Anthony, let's.'

They went up the stairs, and sat on the stairs. They were quite alone.

'Look here, Diane, I don't love you.'

'Oh, Anthony, I'm so glad. I really am.' Hand business.

'But, Diane, that isn't all. I love somebody else. Diane, I have to tell you, but you must think me a terrible beast.'

'But why should I, Anthony dear? You don't think I mind, do you?'

'No, I knew you wouldn't mind, but I just had to tell you. Let's go down and dance.' They went.

'What's she called?' asked Diane.

'Mercedes,' said Anthony. 'She's Spanish. It's funny we should both fall to Spain, isn't it?'

'Do you see a lot of her? Does she live in Town?'

'Oh, yes, she lives in Town.'

'What part?'

'Oh – in Kensington.'

'Why? Just about here?'

'Yes, it is really. Only more the other side of Kensington.'

'Is she frightfully pretty?'

'Oh, yes. Well, you know what one thinks when one's in love. You know, she's got a wonderful sort of Spanish beauty. You know what these Spanish people can be. "Full of the warm south", and all that.'

'Who introduced you to her?'

'Oh! A cousin of mine, as a matter of fact.'

'I should rather like to meet her.'

'Well, why not?'

'Yes, Anthony, let's!'

'Well, she's rather rushed at present.'

'What with?'

'Oh, I dunno. She has an awful lot of calls to make, working at a Charity Concert or something.'

'Where at?'

'Oh, the Albert Hall or something.'

'I always said you'd fall in love with somebody else, didn't I, Anthony?'

'Yes, Diane. You've won.'

Anthony left the ball-room and ran quickly up the stairs to his room.

'Oh, God!' said Anthony. 'I think I'll go down to Brighton.'

II

Anthony didn't go down to Brighton, though he saw next to nothing of Diane in the following days. Each joined different laughing groups in the lounge, and were the very best laughers of their groups. They laughed at each other right across the lounge . . .

But he saw her always, alone, just before dinner in front of the blazing lounge fire. A mutual warming of hands and absent talk.

Diane never failed him for this. Anthony would let the gong sound, watch all the people slowly go chatting into dinner, till there was a deep hush in the lounge. Then he waited by the fire.

Soon came the hollow sound of high heels knocking on the stone floor of the hall outside. The heels trod, hard and relentless, on Anthony's heart. The big door opened, creaking, and Diane came to Anthony.

It was only absent talk for five minutes. One large flame lit all her face, and quivered about.

III

Tuesday was New Year's Day. Anthony was going to start life on Tuesday. It had taken a little time to determine whether he would start life on Tuesday, or on the Monday after the day Diane was married.

There was no possible doubt about Diane's marrying now. Anthony had seen Ramon. He came into the hotel one night and kept apart with Diane. He was a fine-featured, dark, black-eyed young man of about twenty-six, with triangular trousers, slim waist, gaudy linen, and a splendid ring on his little finger. 'Did you see Ramon last night?' asked Diane at their little before-dinner meeting the next evening. 'Yes. Was that him?' 'Yes. What do you think of him?' 'Oh, he looked awfully good looking.'

On and after Tuesday Anthony was going to get ahead with being a great novelist and a great actor. In the mornings he was going to visit theatrical agents; in the evenings he was going to write, deep into the night, at his novel. A thick manuscript, typed at last. A book, with coloured illustrated wrapper, and deep print on thick pages . . .

But before he started life on Tuesday he was going to have a Wild Night – a Wild Night to conclude his nineteen years of muddled folly and laziness, to help him to forget.

The Wild Night was fixed for New Year's Eve. On that night Mrs Egerton was giving yet another Dinner and Dance – the final, overwhelming, Fancy Dress, New Year's Eve, Dance. At ten Anthony set out from the Fauconberg for Piccadilly. The dance had just started. He met Diane on the stairs, going up to it, just as he was going out.

IV

He was at Piccadilly at half-past ten, and morosely started his Wild Night.

He stayed where the lifts come up into Jermyn Street. The usual girls and women passed him, looking ahead of them in the old way, as though they were having their photographs taken and finding it rather fun. But Anthony couldn't bring himself to respond. He went down the Haymarket. 'It's no good. I can't do it. Nothing'll ever make me forget Diane.'

'Oh, God, if only I could die,' said Anthony. 'If only I could die, now, in her arms ...'

And then he found himself saying 'Good-evening' to a girl, and raising his hat, and wondering if it was done to raise one's hat.

'Good-evening,' she said, and leant her head back to look up at him.

'Let's go up here', said Anthony for something to say, pointing to the Circus.

Nothing was said for quite half a minute. 'It's getting beastly cold tonight, isn't it?' said Anthony.

'Yes, it is,' she said, with a voice ever so homely. 'And it was so lovelee earlier in the day, wasentit?'

'Yes. But then this beastly climate always is like that.'

'Yes, it is, isentit? I'm going to America soon.'

'Oh, are you? It's better there. This climate's awful. They say that's why the English are such good colonisers. They can sort of stand anything after this. I say, where are we going? Let's take a taxi.'

They stopped a passing taxi. 'Where *are* we going?' asked Anthony. She gave an address to the taxi man.

They crossed Piccadilly with many stoppages. Anthony looked out of the window.

Suddenly he turned his face to her and looked very shocked indeed. 'Good lord!' he said. 'I've just remembered a terribly urgent appointment. I say. I must go. Look here, will you pay this man? I'll get out here. I really must go. He's coming to a stop again all right. I'll give you the money and you pay him.' He gave her three crisp pound-notes. 'So long.' Anthony stumbled out into the street.

'Damn! Damn!' he said. 'An appointment! An appointment! Hell! Why the hell didn't I go through with it? Three pounds. An appointment! Remembered a terribly urgent appointment! Oh, God!' Unspeakable invective.

He walked up Regent Street. A wind was rising now, and he was cold. He walked down Regent Street and took a train to Earl's Court.

V

The ball-room was very full – the old beautiful, moving kaleidoscope of rich, gay, clean colours. Diane was in black evening dress. She danced with a Sicilian Brigand, perhaps. Her eyes did nothing while she danced. There was just the natural bitter droop of the mouth.

The dance ended. Diane saw Anthony at the door and came to him. 'Hullo, Anthony.' Forlornly said.

'Hullo, Diane. Can I have the next dance?'

'Yes. Certainly.'

Three minutes' waiting about and off-hand criticism of the dresses. The band started again and Diane and Anthony went on to the floor.

'Diane dear, let's sit this out.'

'Yes – let's, Anthony.'

VI

They went up the stairs and sat on them. They were quite alone. The music came through softly.

'Look here, Diane. I'm going to make an orderly confession to you, and you've got to hear the whole of it before you answer.'

'But why?'

'Well, first of all, Diane, I love you. I always have loved you and always will love you till the end of all things.

Really, Diane. My whole life's given up to you, Diane, really it is.'

'But, Anthony—'

'Shut up, Diane. I don't mean shut up, Diane, but shut up. You've got to listen to me. You know, like heroes in cheap dramas who say, 'No, by God, you shall hear me out!' Diane. I've always loved you, not for your beauty or anything like that, but because of you, Diane. Diane, don't you remember that night you came to me just before my aunt died? You seemed like a sort of angel. *You* know – a real angel ...

'But Mercedes?' asked Diane, softly, but doggedly.

'Oh, Diane, do shut up. Mercedes was just an invention to save my rotten pride when you said you were going to be married. Where was I? Look here, Diane, don't marry this man Raymond or whatever his rotten name is. He looks an awful cad. Really he does. Wait a little, Diane. Just a little. You'd be frightfully miserable. And it's madness to marry at your age. Think of it, Diane. You've got to be with him all your life. *You* know, breakfast every morning and all that. And he looks an awful beast. Really he does, Diane. Now look here, if you married me it'd be wonderful, because you know I'd love you far more than anybody else could. And it wouldn't be like an ordinary marry – marriage, because I'd understand. You wouldn't have to see more of me than you wanted and it'd be wonderful. Really it would, Diane.'

Anthony rose on that. His mouth was trembling and

bitter. Diane rose too, put her hands round Anthony's shoulders in a very clever way, and her protesting mouth on Anthony's bitter mouth.

Then Diane put Anthony away from her, and said, 'Let's sit down and talk again, Anthony; I've got something to tell you.'

'What, Diane?'

A lady came up the stairs. 'Oh, how you people must hate me,' said the lady. 'Not a bit of it,' said Diane.

'What do you mean, Diane?'

'All right, Anthony, sit down again, and I'll tell you.'

They sat down.

'To begin with, Ramon doesn't exist,' she said. 'He's my cousin.'

'Look here, Anthony, I did know that Mercedes didn't exist.'

'Diane? Did you?'

'Well, of course, I wasn't sur-ur-re, Anthony.' She spoke in the amiable and interested tone proper to the *dénouement*. 'But you weren't a bit convincing, and you did get so frightfully muddled when I asked you where she lived and all that.

'I wasn't really going to be married a bit,' continued Diane, as though you could take that sacrament in various degrees. 'But I was so frightfully fed up after your note from Cheltenham that I simply had to say I was. And you kept on about Mercedes, so I kept on about Ramon. You know, Anthony, I knew all the time you were frightfully in love.'

'Not "in love",' said Anthony. 'Love.'

'Yes, Love, Anthony dear. Anyway, I was waiting for you to do something like this, and I'm terribly glad it's come.'

The lady returned down the stairs. 'I'm still at it,' said the lady. 'Not at all,' said Diane.

'That's all, Anthony.'

'Diane.'

'Yes.'

'Diane, do you think you could ever love me at all?'

'Look here, Anthony, I do love you,' said Diane, and blushed. 'And I understand all that you mean about everything, and I do love you.'

'Oh, Diane dear, do you mean it? Do you know what it means, Diane? Oh, Diane, this is wonderful. Wonderful? What a word. Diane!'

And Anthony was kissing her again.

VII

Diane and Anthony sat in the dining-room. Their eyes were bright and clear, and each held a glass of clear lemonade, sipping it very slowly.

'We'll get married, won't we, Diane?'

'Yes, rather.'

'But we don't want to get married quickly, do we, Diane? We've got the rest of our lives together, so what does it matter?'

'Exactly.'

'As a matter of fact, when I'm twenty-one I get quite a decent amount of money. It works out at about eight pounds a week. Could we marry on that?'

'Oh, easily.'

'Oh, Diane, you are wonderful. But, of course, I'll have made pots of money before then. You see, I'll be able to really start now. Oh, I say, Diane, we won't have any comic children or anything, will we?'

'No, Anthony.'

Diane had to leave Anthony when they went up to dance. A Knight Templar (in all probability) claimed a neglected dance from her. But Diane and Anthony were happy in getting away from each other. There was nothing better than to see each other maintaining the old commonplace attitude to the old people, just as though the great thing hadn't happened. They talked about dresses, and dancing, and New Year's Eves, and weather with quite silly enthusiasm, and at the poorest jest Anthony gave a rich, golden laugh.

And just before twelve Mrs Egerton came, like a queen, down to her dance. She was not like a queen because she was arrayed as Elizabeth of England – but because she kept one hand on the other in front of her, and smiled, and everybody praised her, and looked at her, and to her, and thanked her for the Dance. And it was *her* Dance. And everybody said that her dress was far and away the best, and that she ought to dance with Mr Kingston (Sir Walter Raleigh, possibly), and one person bowed low before her.

And there was a hint of royalty in the way the Punch almost immediately followed Mrs Egerton. The Punch was brought in on silver salvers by four servants who were just going off to a dance of their own.

There was just an inappreciable stoppage when a streamer hit Mrs Egerton full in the face, and hurt her, and got all tangled in her tiara ('They really shouldn't be so rough, should they?' she said), but the truth was that nobody really cared two pins about Mrs Egerton, and she soon forgot it, and made them all join hands and form a circle for 'Auld Lang Syne'.

This was a bawling, tumultuous affair. Only a few people and Mrs Egerton knew the words, but they all shouted. Anthony made do with 'O *old* langzine, o *old* langzine; o old, o old langzine. O old, o old, o old, o old, o old, o old LANGZINE!'

Then they all crowded on to the balcony of the Fauconberg, and hushed awhile, breathing audibly, and whispering threats to the giggling Betty, till they heard the distant hurrying bells coming through the air of the cold, clear night. Three cheers and some more dancing.

Anthony kept by Diane now, and asked her to dance so

soon after the band struck up each time that no one else could get a look in and ask her.

And that was a very good game, and in the intervals of the dancing Anthony had another game – the game of 'Hold Mrs Egerton's flowing train while she talks to Mr Kingston.'

'No – you mustn't,' said Diane. 'No – really, Anthony. No. You mustn't. No. It's rude.'

'It's not rude,' said Anthony. 'I'm a train-bearer.'

At last the dancing came to be rather the same, and dullish. Anthony said to Diane, 'Let's escape and go out for a walk.'

They put on coats and things and went quietly out of the front door.

'Come on, Diane de Poictiers.'

'Diane de *Poictiers*,' repeated Diane, with scorn.

'Who *was* Diane de Poictiers?'

'I dunno. Where are we going, Anthony?'

'Oo, the Albert Hall, to see Mercedes at the Charity Concert.'

'Yes, Anthony. Or to Ramon's house outside New York. Though as a matter of fact there is one . . .'

'Yes, Diane, you weren't nearly such a bad liar as me— I. Ramon did nearly exist.'

'Yes. But he did not – exist – in – that – catter*goary*. Catter*goary*. Catter*goary*?'

'*Category*.'

'*Category*? Category, *cat*egory, *cat*egory, *cat*egory, *cat*egory'

'Not too much on the *cat*. Oh, Diane, it was frightfully sentimental and Tennysony of me, but it was wonderful to hear those clear bells and to think of the new year, and all that.'

'Yes, Anthony. I know.'

The street might have been rich silver, made for them. They passed a yellow, flaring coffee-stall, they passed a young man talking earnestly and quietly to a woman at the top of some area steps, and they passed a policeman, who took no notice of them. They went on aimlessly through the clear, resounding Squares, and Diane's cold, funny hand was in Anthony's great-coat pocket.

Once they passed two drunk men. 'Let us weigh the matter out,' said one drunk man to the other. 'You're good fellow, but let us weigh the matter out.'

Diane and Anthony slipped around a corner. 'You wait till we're married, Diane, I'll come back miles worse than that ....'

To buy any of our books and to find out
more about Abacus and Little, Brown, our authors
and titles, as well as events and book clubs,
visit our website

www.littlebrown.co.uk

and follow us on Twitter

@AbacusBooks
@LittleBrownUK